Joseph Cook, Newell Dunbar, Frederic William Farrar

Phillips Brooks

The Man, the Preacher, and the Author

Joseph Cook, Newell Dunbar, Frederic William Farrar

Phillips Brooks
The Man, the Preacher, and the Author

ISBN/EAN: 9783337146122

Printed in Europe, USA, Canada, Australia, Japan

Cover: Foto ©Raphael Reischuk / pixelio.de

More available books at **www.hansebooks.com**

PHILLIPS BROOKS:

THE MAN, THE PREACHER, AND THE AUTHOR.

BASED ON THE "ESTIMATE"
BY NEWELL DUNBAR.

WITH AN INTRODUCTION BY JOSEPH COOK,

AND A

SUPPLEMENTARY CHAPTER FROM

THE VEN. FREDERICK W. FARRAR, D.D.,
ARCHDEACON AND CANON OF WESTMINSTER.

TO WHICH ARE ADDED

SELECTIONS FROM THE WRITINGS OF
THE LATE GREAT DIVINE.

PROFUSELY ILLUSTRATED WITH PORTRAITS
AND VIEWS OF THE SCENES OF
HIS LIFE AND LABORS.

BOSTON:
JOHN K. HASTINGS.
OFFICE OF "THE CHRISTIAN,"
47 AND 49 CORNHILL.
1893.

To the Admirers of

Trne Manhood

this little volume is lovingly dedicated
by the Author.

PHILLIPS BROOKS.

Great bishop, greater preacher, greatest man,
  Thy manhood far out-towered all church, all
    creed,
  And made thee servant of all human need,
Beyond one thought of blessing or of ban,
Save of thy Master, whose great lesson ran: —
  "The great are they who serve." So now, indeed,
  All churches are one church in loving heed
Of thy great life wrought on thy Master's plan!
As we stand in the shadow of thy death,
  How petty all the poor distinctions seem
    That would fence off the human and divine!
Large was the utterance of thy living breath;
    Large as God's love this human hope and dream;
    And now humanity's hushed love is thine!

Minot J. Savage.

A Message from Phillips Brooks.

✠

I LOOK round on the work to do, and I do not believe that either Episcopalianism or Methodism or Presbyterianism or Baptism is going to assert the victory of Christianity over sin, the opening of the barred citadel of wickedness in this our land. The Church of Christ, simple, unimpeded, armed powerfully because armed lightly, the essential Church of Christ, must make the first entrance. Then let us have up our methods of denominational government, and each, in the way that he thinks most divine, strive for the perfected dominion of our one great Lord.

INTRODUCTION.

I.

ROBERTSON, Raphael, Byron, Burns, died each at thirty-seven. Phillips Brooks had more years than Napoleon, or Schiller, or Abraham Lincoln. In the cathedral of God's completed providences there are no unfinished or broken columns.

Nevertheless, the pathos of Phillips Brooks's life was in its withheld completion. He died at what had seemed to the world to be his mid-day. He was maturing to the last. His published pages are a precious and perpetual legacy. He probably performed as many hours of important labor in his fifty-seven years as most men do in seventy. His balanced soul was as remarkable for sense as for sensitiveness, for sym-

metry as for size, for humility and spirituality as for surcharge of life and
aspiration.   But he has left nothing behind him which represents adequately
his magnificent depth of character, or
his unexplored reserves of growth.

II.

QUANTITY of being, amplitude of natural endowment, richness of emotional,
intellectual, and spiritual power were
what impressed men most in Phillips
Brooks.   He was in every way a large
man, and in almost no sense fragmen-
tary or fractional.   An orator easily addresses every side of human nature that
he possesses. Phillips Brooks had a
many-sided soul.   It is the simple fact
that he was especially skilled in the
knowledge, because he was himself opulent in the possession, of the loftier and
nobler sides of human endowment.   A
polygonal nature is usually a powerful
nature ; but a spherical yet more so.
Size without symmetry may mean mis-
chief. Phillips Brooks had both size
and symmetry, both sensitiveness and
spirituality, and so was remarkable for
quality as well as for quantity of being.
Even his commanding physical presence
was a palpable advantage to him in his

public work. He was unconscious of the
fact, but others were not. Culture did
what it could for him ; birth did more.
Culture in the family, the Boston school,
Harvard University, the theological hall
at Alexandria, the toil of his life, did
not make his size, nor his symmetry —
they did not unmake them.

III.

As to the matter and manner of the
most inspiring of the discourses of Phillips Brooks, their charm and power con-
sist largely in the fact that he was a
geographer of spiritual uplands. His
delight in picturing the higher experi-
ences of the soul was as profound as
his skill in doing so was remarkable.
He almost never spoke of himself, but
he had in his own nature and experience
the spiritual uplands which he described.
His most characteristic sermons are
maps of highlands of religious life and
truth. But they are more than maps.
He was an excellent, though not always
a methodical, surveyor of these elevated
regions, and could produce accurate outline charts of them by a few bold
strokes. But his discourses have their
power, not so much in their outlines as
in their sunlight and atmosphere. Ver-

IV.

PHILLIPS BROOKS was the prophet of
the Parable of the Prodigal Son.   His
discourses continually emphasize the
organizing and redemptive doctrines of
the Fatherhood of God, and the sonship
of men.   He was the apostle of the in-
dwelling God.   His watchword was not
so much the Cross as the immanent Im-
manuel.   Every human being, although
a prodigal, is yet a son, and may be expected to return to his Father's house.
Phillips Brooks did not often, but he
did sometimes, emphasize the Scriptural
truth that there are prodigals of whom
we have no evidence that they will ever
return.   The reconciling kiss is not
given to prodigals actually in rebellion.
Of this latter fact Phillips Brooks said
little, but there is, of course, no doubt
that he believed it.   (See his remarkable discourses entitled "The Law of
Liberty" and " An Evil Spirit from the
Lord.")

Mr. Gladstone called Frederick Deni-
son Maurice a spiritual splendor.   John
Stuart Mill said of Maurice that he
was the only preacher he knew who
had brains enough and to spare.   Phillips Brooks often spoke of Maurice as

a theological author to whom he owed a vast debt. Every one familiar with Maurice's life and system of thought will see that he, more than any one else, except perhaps Stanley and Robertson, stood near to Phillips Brooks. Their views of broad church doctrine and polity were almost identical. Phillips Brooks's emphasis, or omission of emphasis, on certain doctrines is almost the same with theirs. Those who think the latter somewhat incomplete in their view of several vital Christian truths may think the former so.

Although Bishop Brooks was an optimist and a broad churchman, it is certain that he was a consistent Episcopalian. It is very unfair to assert that he held Unitarian or Universalist views of Christian truth. It has been well said of him that he was liberal-minded, but not a liberal.

He had around him, as he himself said, four concentric circles — that of his own church nearest, but next that of Christendom, next that of religious humanity, lastly, that of the whole human race. In his native Commonwealth there was a sense in which he was Bishop of us all.

V.

LET a statue be erected in Copley Square representing Phillips Brooks in his preacher's robes, but let the posture and look of it be such as to lead all beholders to think of his message even more than of the man. If we wish to act in his spirit, let us reverence the truths he taught more than the teacher himself. The statue should look upward. No portrait of him that I have ever seen gives adequate expression to his best look — that solar light which came to his countenance in his most elevated and rapt moods. St. Gaudens, whose *Puritan* at Springfield and *Lincoln* at Chicago are unmatched among American statues, will succeed in such a work. On the four sides of the pedestal ought to stand words of his own, like these : —

On the North Side.

"The freeing of souls is the judging of souls. A liberated nature dictates its own destiny."

On the East Side.

"Man is a son of God, on whom the Devil has laid his hand, and not a child of the Devil whom God is trying to steal."

On the West Side.

"That book is most inspired which most worthily and deeply tells the story of the most inspired life."

On the South Side.

"The Divine in us reaches upward, and the Divine above reaches downward, and the two mingle; and that is a living faith in a living Christ."

No statue can fitly represent Phillips Brooks unless in figure, face and atmosphere it proclaims the Divine Immanence in the human soul, the Fatherhood of God and the brotherhood of men.

JOSEPH COOK.

BOSTON, Feb. 6, 1893.

CONTENTS.

CHAPTER		PAGE

ILLUSTRATIONS.

Together with Head *and* Tail Pieces.

PERSONALITY.

Yours very sincerely
Phillips Brooks

NOTE.

THE first five chapters of the Biographical portion of this volume are taken, by permission of the author, from " An Estimate of Phillips Brooks," by Newell Dunbar. They were written during the great preacher's lifetime, which accounts for the use in them of the present tense. Chapters vi., vii., viii., ix., and x. were written after his death.

I.

PERSONALITY.

THE man (or woman) of this world has been spoilt by the world. He has given himself over to standards and methods of which the sum and substance are selfishness, and has allowed himself to grow — to state the plain truth — into a repulsive monstrosity. Himself he regards in the light of all but a deity to be worshiped ; upon his fellows he looks about to see how best he can make use of them. He has drifted far from

and reversed the healthy instincts of
his childhood and of Nature. The
scholar (signifying by that term the
man or woman, who is not merely
a receptacle for facts, but who has
thought and aspired in those broader
and deeper and more life-giving, if
less exact, departments of intellectual endeavor — the theologies, the
philosophies, the poesies, the æsthet-
ics, of the intellectual *curriculum* — of
which the prerogative is that they
tend to decipher the meaning of
life and to give it an unrest, a
self-dissatisfaction, a distinctively
human charm, and a worthy aim)
has at least *considered* the "what
ought to be," as well as the "what
is." He feels its superiority.

When, as occasionally happens, he is true to his teaching, and is besides, in addition to being a scholar, a man of strong will and of virile powers, making up his mind he will never desert that which he knows in his heart to be the higher for what he equally by intuition knows is the lower, he achieves some appreciable measure of success in embodying the ideal in his own life, and in causing it to be embodied in the life about him. Such men constitute the flower of our race. And it is, in the first place, to be noted of them, that they represent normal and con-sistent growths of humanity, are not vitiated or warped, but such as

Nature intended human nature to be; the man not contradicting the boy, but continuing him — *containing* the boy — the boy grown up — a *bigger* boy — combining all the youth's simple, true, generous instincts, and all-embracing sympathies and affections, with the man's added stature, strength, polish, knowledge, culture, and wisdom. Says Novalis: "*Tugend ist die Prosa, Unschuld die Poesie.*"

Such a man eminently is Phillips Brooks. Those who have had the privilege of knowing him intimately have often styled him a "big boy." The scholar, the high-bred gentleman, the man of weight and of influence upon the community about

him, if not, indeed, in the world;
but beneath all simple, unaffected,
modest, hopeful, trustful, unselfish
and well-wishing. It needs but to
see him upon the tennis-ground with
children, or in his church on a
" children's day," to recognize the
peculiar aptness of the epithet
alluded to above. Its truthfulness
no doubt accounts in large measure
for his influence with the young,
especially with young men, it being
a notorious fact that amongst
preachers he is the darling of American universities. Those who have
beheld that vast surpliced frame in
Trinity Church chancel drop upon
its knees and lift up its voice in
all the artless effusion of unques-

tioning prayer, have the key to the man. There is nothing studied, or affected, or done for effect, or *sham*, about him. He is natural and genuine, and fundamental (in the sense of clinging to and embodying the great underlying facts — the first principles — of life and of our common human nature), and true. That here is a genuine man, human through and through, and with all his elegance and cultivation at heart one with humanity, one with the *people*, no one could question after reading his sermon preached in the church of the Holy Trinity, Philadelphia, after the assassination of President Lincoln — it is so gloriously adequate to its high theme.

No one could so speak, no one could so appreciate the simple grandeur of character of that remarkable man, and not be himself compact of true manhood.

In his Boston Latin School oration, he praises the school because its teaching has never been "the privilege of an aristocratic class, but the portion of any boy in town who had the soul to desire it and the brain to appropriate it." A fact that indubitably attests the authenticity of his metal is that, whenever he preaches or speaks to what might be termed the populace, the populace eagerly listen to him. Just as the gipsies and poachers were Charles Kingsley's friends, styling him their "priest-king," the lower ranks of American society flock to hear Phillips Brooks, whenever they get the chance, equally with the more critical classes. They seem to be equally abject subjects of his spell : and as between reality and sham the populace in any country possess a very keen vision, that in the long run nothing spurious cheats. His "eye is single,"—one evidence of this trait being his deliberate determination to lead a celibate life, in order to devote himself the more completely to his sacred calling. Mr. Drummond, in one of his recent books, speaks of the fine opportunity afforded by the Christian ministry for devoting one's self to a high ideal, undistracted by the disturbing element of money, which is so potent a factor in most other callings. Narrowness of means, indeed, Bishop Brooks has been spared; but no one can doubt it would have made no difference to his zeal, whatever it might have done to his effectiveness, if he had not been; certainly in choosing his profession he was not actuated by mercenary motives.

To have his name in the mouths of the community, and to have the community's gratitude express itself in gifts, have fallen to him naturally; but they have made no difference in the man.

As it happens to almost every

one in Boston, at one time or another,
to meet him with his burly frame
and big eloquent eye upon the
streets, where he may be seen hustled
like any ordinary mortal by hack-
men and porters, who are apparently
perfectly unconcerned and unconscious that they are rubbing elbows
with a great man (or, perhaps, even
exhibit a somewhat overdone assump-
tion and bravado of ignorance or of
self-assertion, as is wont to be the
way with the low-class American);
or running across him occasionally
in a book-shop, with his face buried
in a volume in rapt and scholarly
abstraction; or finding him a near
neighbor in the audience at some
public place of amusement, or listen-

ing with fine modesty in the audience or congregation to the eloquence of another — even the most careless observer may notice in him a certain noble intentness of countenance, and a sober restriction of regard, that bespeak the genuine unspoilt nature, self-centred in the sense of being loyally wedded to and humbly dependent upon the revelation of the highest within.

Very characteristic of the man was a little scene the writer remembers to have witnessed, one evening in early summer, on the Commonwealth Avenue mall in Boston. The great preacher was sauntering down the walk in earnest converse with a friend, or at least acquaintance, whose hand he held in his, and was affectionately swinging as he talked —just as children swing hands and talk. His companion, who was known to the writer as a man notoriously not *all* unworldly and a saint, though of average size, looked a mere boy beside his own heroic proportions. Brooks was expostulating with him in regard to some point on which he evidently wished to change him, and his big, convincing, *winning*, "Nonsense — nonsense, Edward — put it aside — you *know* it is not so," sounded very hard to resist. It is not always argument with him, but oftentimes the pressure brought to bear of a well-nigh irresistible magnetism and potent personality.

WILLIAM GRAY BROOKS—FATHER OF PHILLIPS BROOKS.

It is amusingly told of him (and it illustrates the modesty of the man) by one of his clergy, who is rector of a suburban Boston parish, and in whose church he frequently preaches — on which occasions the pews overflow, settees are placed in the aisles, and all the available interstices are occupied by people standing — that always, after the service, he says, with the utmost good faith, " Grey, what a splendid congregation you have ! " It apparently never enters his head to imagine that that is not the usual condition of things in that church, when preachings are afoot.

Another story told of him by his friend Archdeacon Farrar illustrates the same trait. When wonder was

expressed, during one of his English
visits, by some of his English friends,
at the generous, if unaccepted, offer
made to him by certain members of
his congregation at home, to send
him abroad for a year, paying all
his expenses and those of a substitute during his absence, he answered
laughing, "Oh, they were tired of
me, and wanted a change!"

Any reference to the personality
of Phillips Brooks would be incomplete without some allusion to
his *physique*. To be not only big
morally and intellectually, but well-
nigh herculean bodily, constitutes a
sort and condition of man that is
eminently adapted for reaching all
classes in the community — both

those who appreciate the higher spiritual graces, those who delight mainly in hard-headedness, and lastly the more purely animal, upon whose lowness of grade moral and mental adornments are quite thrown away, but who recognize and respect good tangible thews and bulk when they see them. When the apostle of mercy and forbearance comes, it is well for him to come, if possible, equipped in this Milonian fashion: for one thing, he can scarcely then be suspected of preaching what he practices from necessity and from motives of interest.

Like all thoroughly healthy natures, Phillips Brooks at once detects and hates flattery. Intelligent appreciation is welcome to him, as it must be to every genuine man. The outside world exists for him as something to be benefited : for its adulation he does not seem to care, preferring for society that of his intimate friends, with whom he is sunshine itself. Of himself he speaks little. His sense of humor is strong, as any one for instance may see by reading the delicious oration delivered at the celebration of the two-hundred-and-fiftieth anniversary of the founding of the Boston Latin School, which has already been referred to. Nobody seems to know when he does his work : he is always accessible and disengaged in the morning. He is very optimistic, believing in the intrinsic goodness of human nature. He thinks that the world makes steady progress in accordance with a fixed law. His principal regret is that he cannot live longer, since he is convinced that at about the time when the next generation shall have fairly taken its place upon the scene and settled down to work, there will occur a sudden blossoming out in the condition of humanity such as it has never before beheld.

How shall the personality of Phillips Brooks be summed up? Archdeacon Farrar calls him "every inch a man." To the writer recur the words Brooks himself spoke of Lincoln (so different from himself till you get down to the very core of the two men) — "the greatness of real goodness, and the goodness of real greatness".

BIOGRAPHICAL.

II.

BIOGRAPHICAL.

THE Right Reverend Phillips Brooks, D.D., Harv., Bishop of Massachusetts, and today doubtless the greatest preacher in America or in England, if not of Protestantism and of the world, was born in Boston, December 13, 1835, and is consequently now in his fifty-sixth year He is in the full vigor of a regally-endowed manhood, and likely to be able to devote many years to come to the causes of religion and of education which he has held so dear. The original home of his family was North Andover. That his parents were devoted to Christianity, appears from the fact that of their six sons four, including him, became Christian ministers. When he was a boy, the family attended St. Paul's Church, in Boston, of which the rector was that admirable pulpit-orator, the Rev. Alexander Hamilton Vinton, whose polished eloquence, it is not unnatural to suppose, may have had considerable influence in arousing in young Brooks's heart that predominant ideal which so often makes the boy in a great sense father of the man. Dr. Vinton afterwards for a second time, as will be seen later, exerted a beneficent influence upon his young friend, and at a critical point in his life. Dr. Vinton, by the way, preached the con-secration-sermon at the consecra-tion of the new Trinity Church, Boston.

Young Brooks fitted for college at the Boston Latin School, and in 1851 was admitted to Harvard University, by which famous in-stitution he was duly graduated in 1855, being then in his nineteenth year.

It is on record that at about the time of his graduation — that criti-cal period in the lives of educated youth — he was in doubt (as so many such young men are) what profession to adopt. When stil. a senior he consulted the President of his University on the point, and that learned gentleman, with all the omniscient insight of a very wise man, said: "In deciding the difficult question of a choice of profession, I think, we may always be helped towards a solution of the problem by eliminating, in the first place, the *impossible* vocations. This saves much trouble and loss of time, as it at once narrows the field, and restricts the mind to fewer points, from which to make its selection. Now, in your case, for instance, owing to the impediment in your speech, you could

never be a *preacher*, and we may
as well therefore at the outset lay
aside all thought of the ministry."
Just what profession collegiate in-
fallibility recommended its young
applicant for advice to adopt, need
not be recalled here: the irony of
subsequent events has extracted
the interest from the rest of the
little oration.   The advice given
was no doubt sound, judging from
the standpoint of probability, and
weighing what seemed to be the
chances.   Moreover, the speaker,
beyond a doubt, gave it with reluc-
tance, as his preferences must all
have been in favor of the pulpit.
This very funny story, however,
would never have risen up and lived

to be told against him, if, classical scholar as he was, he had not been temporarily oblivious of the paradoxical case, upwards of two thousand years ago, of a certain somewhat famous man in Athens, named Demosthenes. The wreck of his prophecy only furnishes one more proof, what unforeseen and wonderful things a great personality, in "dead earnest," unaccountably manages to achieve.

In spite of the well-meant advice of the sagacious but *human* President, the future preacher decided to make the ministry his life-calling; and, in order to prepare himself for it, betook himself to the Episcopal Divinity School at

Alexandria, Va., graduating here in 1859. Many are the recollections of his noble character and promise cherished by those who were his classmates here. Here it was that he wrote his first sermon, on "The simplicity that is in Christ," of which he himself — his sense of humor being keen, even when he himself is the victim — recounts that a classmate's criticism of it was, "There was very little simplicity in it, and no Christ."

If graduating from college is the Saarbrück in a young man's career, graduating from his professional school is his Sedan. The perplexing question of establishing himself, and of making a start, then confronts

him.   In this respect, indeed, the
young minister has the advantage
over the young lawyer and the
young doctor. Unless the latter have
some means of subsistence apart
from their professions, the outlook
for them is disheartening, indeed:
in all probability, it will be years
before their position is secure, and
their practice remunerative.   The
"starting" clergyman, on the other
hand, as soon as he has secured a
parish at all, at once secures with
it a living, and a place for making
himself felt.   But with a young
man of large possibilities, how great
the importance where and what
that first parish is!   If it be off by
comparison somewhere in the back-
woods, with a scant, commonplace
and insignificant congregation, in
all human likelihood, to be sure, he

will work to the front, and win the
position suited to his powers, in time ;
but it will probably take him years
to do so, and when the opportunity shall have been conquered,
youth will have fled, and the
momentum and keenness of his first
onset have been dulled.   Phillips
Brooks's first parish was the Church
of the Advent, in Philadelphia, of
which he became rector in 1859. The
story of his settlement here constitutes quite a little romance, — one of
those fascinating romances of genius
with which the biographies of eminent men present us.   At the Advent, his preaching and character at
once made themselves felt ; but,
though in a general way it may be
said that the intellectual grade of
nearly *all* Episcopal parishes is high,
still by comparison the congregation

was composed mainly of plain people,
the church edifice was in an obscure
quarter of the city, and the opportunity afforded for the rector to become
widely-known was small.   It was just
at this point that Dr. Vinton — who
had in the meantime become the rector of the large, wealthy and growing
Church of the Holy Trinity, in Philadelphia — rendered the essential service spoken of above.   He opened his
pulpit to young Brooks Sunday after-
noons : the results being that the Advent presently began to overflow
Sunday mornings with Holy Trinity
parishioners, and that when Dr. Vinton removed to New York soon afterward the rector of the Advent was
invited to take his place. After being
thrice asked, Brooks was installed
rector of Holy Trinity in 1862 ; thus,
with few tedious preliminaries, quickly

stepping into a first-rate position in a great and populous city. Here his fame as a preacher grew, and came to extend far beyond the warm-hearted Quaker City, and indeed beyond its State. In Philadelphia, he remained ten years, and departed thence greatly regretted, leaving behind him a memory such as it has been given to but few men to create. Whenever he returns thither on a visit, his welcome resembles that of the prodigal son.

When young Brooks was seeking his first parish, his native city of Boston — in regard to whom, her critics have not been slow in pointing out how frequently she has failed to know her greatest — somehow or other did not seem burning with anxiety to furnish him a foothold; but when the noise of him had gone abroad in the land, and it began to be said that Phillips Brooks of Philadelphia was the greatest preacher in the Episcopal Church, if not indeed in the country, Boston — if somewhat tardily — opened her eyes and heart (not forgetting her pocket), and concluded to take him in. Indeed, it has been further remarked by those extremely keen-sighted persons, her critics, that after driving her unrecognized geniuses from her door on penalty if need be of starvation, once let them become of mark elsewhere, and — thrifty Yankee that she is with eye ever roving for the "rising sun" — she hastens to welcome them back.   In 1869 the rector of the Holy Trinity, Philadelphia, received and accepted a call to and became the rector of Trinity Church, Boston.

His new parish, like the one he left, was a strong and influential one. Its church edifice, with "its battlemented tower, like a great castle of the truth," was at that time a conspicuous object in Summer Street. It was destroyed in the "great fire" of 1872. The parish at once proceeded to erect a new place of worship. The plans for it were drawn by that architect of sweetness and light, Mr. H. H. Richardson, — whose untimely death was a loss to American art, — and by all odds the most complete, thoroughly-built and beautiful church-building in the United States, with a seating capacity of over two thousand, situated on Boylston Street in the choicest residential portion of the city, and costing over a million dollars, was the result. For architectural beauty it will compare with many of the famous places of worship, hallowed by time and by sacred memories, of green England. As one regards it in the bright morning or in the early evening light, fancy adds the softening of outline — the mellowing and metamorphosis of tints — the more daring spread of the ivies — that are to come with the years, and the heart, yielding a sigh of deep content, confesses to itself: "It is enough!"

The new church was taken possession of in 1877, and from that time to this has been the home of Phillips Brooks's eloquence. The audiences it has contained have grown with the fame of its rector, till today it often scarcely suffices to admit the throngs that seek entrance. In 1886 he was elected Assistant-Bishop of Pennsylvania, but declined. The offer of a Professorship in Harvard University was also at this time made him; but neither did he accept this.

He has at various times been a quite extensive traveler, having visited no inconsiderable portion of the earth's surface, including India, Palestine and Japan : it may be added that he cherishes the hope of extending his travels before he dies still further. In England his visits have been numerous, and he has made many friends and created a deep impression there. He preached at Westminister Abbey ; at both the Universities ; before the Queen, and before many of the first people in the Kingdom. It was and is the opinion of Archdeacon Farrar, that his equal as a preacher and as a man does not exist amongst the clergy of the English Church.

At the death of Bishop Paddock in

1891, he was almost unanimously elected Bishop in his stead by the Diocese of Massachusetts. According to the very singular, and it is thought wholly unprecedented, arrangement existing in the American Episcopal Church, however, in that church a diocese practically cannot elect its own bishop, the election not being valid until it has been ratified by a majority of all the bishops in the Church. The objections urged against him, the long contest over the matter, and all the sorry tale of innuendo, recrimination and partisan strife, need not be recounted here. They are fresh in the minds of all, and are now happily ended. Even as you are reading this little book its title has been justified, and Phillips Brooks is in fact Bishop of his native State.

THE PREACHER.

III.

THE PREACHER.

ONE need not be very far advanced in life to remember
the time when Curtis, and Willis, and
Emerson, and Lowell, — and many
another illustrious name of that
mighty generation of writers and
speakers, of which today the sur-
vivors are, alas! so few,—were uttering their philippics against the
materiality and sordidness of American life. American life, indeed, has

advanced since then at a giant's pace; it has expanded all round; since its birth, money was never held by it in so high esteem as now; but it has grown in other ways, too. It is not as yet much recognized, in our crude and semibarbaric day, that, great as is its power, money does not give the *best* things, — though that is the fact, seen to be such by the more civilized and sharpest minds. It is an excellent adjunct and accompaniment of the best, but furnishes a poor substitute for it. Did money, for instance, ever yet win a heart? Can it of itself bring happiness? Will it command health? Is anything it ever bought to be com-

Mr. Brooks in his old Room at Alexandria.

FROM A RECENT PHOTOGRAPH.

pared with the joy of the artist, who, day by day, sees grow in visible embodiment beneath his inspired fingers some one of the dreams amongst which his soul habitually dwells, in regions the world wots not of, save as occasionally he vouchsafes it a token from them? With the measureless content of an author, as he pens the last word of a work that he knows will move the hearts and decide the actions of his day, and, when those who make his day shall have vanished, move hearts and influence destinies yet unborn? What within its reach is comparable with the lofty existence, not like unto that of other men, passed by a music-

composer — by Schumann, for instance — amidst celestial harmonies,
whereunto only his ears, and those
of the great tone-gods, are privileged to listen ? With the exultant
sense of beneficent power that
floods and fires the soul of a great
mistress of song — of Christine Nils-
son, say — as she stands before
three thousands of her fellow men
and women, and knows there is not
a tear in all their eyes, a drop of
blood in all their veins, that is not
her slave ? Or of an actor, who
focuses the hearts, with the eyes
and ears, of box, pit and gallery
upon the quiver of an eyelash, the
trembling of a tone ? Or of an
orator, such as Kossuth, or Phillips

or Gough? And of all orators, what one can be likened for unique-ness of position (standing as he does between man and God), for dignity and momentousness of the issues involved, to the orator of the pul-pit — the preacher?

As a preacher — and that, beyond a doubt, is the capacity in which he is greatest — the quality that, in the writer's opinion, first strikes all Phillips Brooks's hearers, is what may perhaps be termed, for lack of a better word, his *copiousness*. He is like a colossal reservoir, that seems full almost to bursting, and well-nigh unable to restrain what it contains. He takes his place in the pulpit, and opens his mouth, and without any accompaniment of manner (whatever may be the case with the matter) specially appropriate to an exordium, just *begins* — right in the middle, as it were. The parting of his lips seems like the bursting open of a safety-valve by the seething thoughts and words behind, and out they rush, so hot in their chase the one of the other, that at times they appear to be almost side by side; and from then till the moment when he stops, with equal abruptness, he simply pours — pours — pours! out — out — out! It seems as if he could not possibly say enough, or begin to express what he has to utter. Just as in his writing, he is superlatively and superbly reckless in lavishing his treasures — apparently feeling that the difficulty is, not to *find* what to say, but to *use* a tithe of the material that throngs and beats and surges to be let out. He gives the *best he has;* never speaking, any more than writing, *down* to the supposed requirements of auditors only partially developed; not stopping to sort, but flinging his words out as they come, satisfied that each hearer will appropriate what belongs to him, and all will get something. Great torrents and waves, as it were, of appeal and aspiration and eloquence and thought rise and fall, and whirl and eddy, throughout the church, till they seem to become almost visible and tangible, and to beat upon the eyes and foreheads of his hearers as they do against their hearts. The audience, caught in the rush and swing of this fervid oratory, feel as if they were rocked upon the impassioned bosom of an ocean of inspired speech. It is soul speaking to soul. Indeed, you have to pay the closest attention, and catch all he says only with difficulty. So rapid and thronging is his utterance that, as is well known, the English reporters, used to a more leisurely eloquence, were at first perplexed and even utterly baffled in their efforts at "taking" him, and finally succeeded in achieving the ability to reach that end only by a sort of special education, obtained through chasing his exceptionally "whirling words." It is to be hoped, by the way, this practice may have had some appreciable effect towards reforming the profession of tachygraphy in Great Britain. Bishop Brooks's oratory has been not inaptly compared to the headlong rush of an express-train.

In point of fact, coolly considered, Phillips Brooks exhibits as a preacher well-nigh every fault of delivery: but he does not leave you time to criticise. There are in him a tremendous vitality, a vigor, an exhaustlessness, an irresistible onset of confident and ardent earnestness, that, whether you will or not, take you clean off your feet, and whirl you along — at their mercy, but pleased, and it is to be hoped benefited. It is not to be wondered at that when Samuel Morley was spending three months in the United States, he stayed over a second Sunday in Boston in order to hear Phillips Brooks preach again.

As to the audiences attracted in his native city and elsewhere by this great American Preacher, they are composed of persons by no means all Episcopalians, but drawn from almost every denomination — some, indeed, having no very distinct religious affiliation or belief of any kind. It seems to have been the case with all the historic preach-ers that their power has sufficed to break the bonds of denomination — thus causing something like a re-turn to the primitive simplicity — and of unbelief. There is something elemental about pulpit utterances of the first rank: they are the lava-stream melting and transfusing all it touches. One who has made a study of the matter is forced to confess that there is good reason for thinking that no inconsiderable number of those who go to hear Phillips Brooks go, less for the sake of any religious instruction or bene-fit to be received, or because they believe what the preacher says, than for the simple purpose of enjoying his oratory — just as they would go to a public place of amusement (a concert, for instance), or to any literary entertainment. Neither probably is this exceptional in his case. It is deeply to be regretted; but looking at the subject inductively, as a matter simply of observation and experience, one is compelled to recognize the fact. This is unfortunately a sceptical and irreligious age, though Americans notoriously admire a man who preëminently "understands his business," and performs it perfectly. Doubtless, Chrysostom never converted *all* his hearers.

If, however, any amongst the audience do not believe what the preacher says, it is simply impossible for any man, woman or child not to believe that the preacher believes it. At those wonderful noonday services in Trinity Church, New York, last year, not one of those clear-headed breathlessly-attentive Wall-Street operators — judges of men trained in perhaps the most sceptical school on earth, and some of them the kings and princes of finance — but knew in his heart by intuition infallible that the speaker before them was a kingly man, who spoke kingly from his soul, and simply *could* not lie, palter, or pretend. They might not in all cases or at all points be able to understand him, but they instinctively knew him to be true. And after all it is impossible to say what chords are genuinely touched, what natures wakened, by pulpit oratory, in spite of themselves, and sometimes even to their own hearts unconfessed. Only He who knows all knows this too. At any moment he who goes to listen from curiosity or to enjoy may find his conscience stung beyond control.

Of the English clergy and their sermons the verse runs —

" They make the best and preach the worst."

Charles Kingsley in the pulpit rested his arm upon or grasped

CHURCH OF THE ADVENT, PHILADELPHIA.

the cushion, meaning to avoid ges-
ticulation ; but as he became aroused,
his eye kindled, his whole frame
vibrated, and with his right hand
he made a curious gesture — which
he seemed unconscious of and unable to restrain—the fingers moving
with a hovering motion like a hawk
about to swoop upon its prey. Car-
dinal Newman in the pulpit re-
sembled a tall, unimpassioned, though
piercingly earnest spectre from another world, with a silvery voice.
Of Whitefield indeed Southey said
his "elocution was perfect" ; he
used to preach each sermon over
and over again, till every inflection
and gesture became perfect. Frank-
lin said he could always tell on

hearing him, from the stage of its finish, how new the sermon was. Bossuet's delivery was dignified yet vehement. Jonathan Edwards stood motionless in the pulpit, one hand resting on it, and the other holding up to his eyes his little closely-written manuscript from which he read. The first sermon Whitefield preached after ordination to the diaconate drove fifteen people insane with fright. When Edwards preached the congregation at times rose to its feet unable to remain sitting, and people fainted. Great men are great *in spite* of their faults. Kingsley had an impediment in his speech, — which disappeared however as soon as he began to speak *in the pulpit*. Whitefield had a cast in one of his eyes. Bossuet's voice was too shrill. All these men succeeded as preachers, as Robertson succeeded, as Brooks succeeds, because they were on fire with holiness to the bottom of their being, and back of their words lay their lives.

THE AUTHOR.

IV.

THE AUTHOR.

WITH perhaps the single exception of two ventures in verse and of his dispassionate paper on "The Episcopal Church" in the "Memorial History of Boston," Bishop Brooks's claims to be considered as an author rest upon his published Sermons, Lectures, and Addresses. Though of course these were written for the purpose of being *delivered*, since they have been made into printed books and given to the public, they may not improperly

be regarded as belonging to the prov-
ince of authorship. Indeed, it might
with some show of justice be urged
that, when he writes *any* of his sermons or addresses, he is in that
act a *writer* — it being only when
he mounts the pulpit or the platform to pronounce them, that he
becomes the *preacher.*

Amongst the strong and well-re-
membered impressions that come
back to one, on turning over the
leaves of the five volumes of Sermons, of the Yale College and of
the Bohlen Lectures, and of
the rest, perhaps the best-remem-
bered and strongest is that of *rich
profusion.* Simile, metaphor, insight ;
historic, scientific, theological and

literary allusion ; observation ; a deep knowledge of human nature — all the wealth of an opulent scholarship and of a teeming brain ; all the riches of an overflowing heart — are proffered without reserve. His learning is worn as a suit of mail-armor, never cramping or stiffening the natural play of his members. Pedantic he never is ; and whenever he employs what may perhaps be styled "library-facts," they have become delightfully metamorphosed : he has put more of himself into the statement than there is of the facts. Indeed he often plays with them — which Goethe thought to be a sign of the master. Especially apt, effective and beautiful are his illustrations, though they are never used for effect, but only as they should be to illustrate. Take one, where a hundred might be given :

"We are like southern plants, taken up to a northern climate and planted in a northern soil. They grow there, but they are always failing of their flowers. The poor exiled shrub dreams by a native longing of a splendid blossom which it has never seen, but it is dimly conscious that it ought somehow to produce. It feels the flower which it has not strength to make in the half-chilled but still genuine juices of its southern nature. That is the way in which the ideal life, the life of full completions, haunts us all."

Such passages as this surely are what even an adversary terms, in the sermons of Luther, "*oasis, pleins de fraîcheur et de poésie, des pensées nobles et délicates, des mouvements pathéthiques et affectueux.*"

His pages bristle with quotable expressions, phrases and sentences of the most striking aptness. As for example : " Faith is the king's knowledge of his own kingship." " A scramble for adherents rather than a Christ-like love for souls." " That first step which costs, we know, cannot be too costly, if it starts the enterprise aright."

The curious thing about a sermon is that, though it is stated logically, the material composing it consists of feeling rather than of thought; and in this respect of *feeling logically handled* Phillips Brooks is unexcelled. He takes a subject and expands it perhaps first, as it were, lengthwise; then laterally; then downwards; and finally upwards to its loftiest reach; adding room after room to the growing edifice, and ever and anon shooting rays of apocalyptic light through it diagonally in every possible direction, till the whole theme stands developed and revealed, vibrating through all its length, and palpitating as it were in all its pores, with a glory of prismatic hues; so to speak, sounding and throbbing even with a music celestial. Sometimes a figure used at the outset of a discourse is repeated or referred to again and again, each reappearance casting a new and wonderful light upon the theme, and marking a fresh step in its growth: as for example the plant and flower illustration in the sermon on "Withheld Completions," or Edom and Judah in the "Conqueror from Edom," which, hinted at and persistently and in greater and greater fullness recurred to throughout, emerge in their complete and overwhelming splendor only at the very end — just as Gounod treats Margaret's apotheosis-theme in "Faust." The beauty and force of these repetitions, occurring often when least expected, and each time strangely like the familiar though changed voice of an unearthly bell knelling out of the sermon's progress, amount at times to a revelation : they attack us in our most defenceless part, in the reason beneath reason, what may be called our "intuitional reason," irresistibly — our tears start, and we cry aloud ! He who has read one of the best of Phillips Brooks's sermons has gazed upon a cartoon drawn — listened to an oratorio composed — by a Great Master of logical and of artistic expression, and of the human heart. Having as it were wafted his reader for half-an-hour through the heavens on rose-tinted clouds, to close sometimes he brings him gently to earth again — in vulgar parlance, "lets him down easy" — in a way that occasionally seems to partake somewhat of anti-climax ;

Phillips Brooks.

FROM A PORTRAIT DURING HIS RECTORSHIP OF THE CHURCH OF THE ADVENT.

although doubtless whenever used it serves the good purpose of leading the audience gradually into harmony with their every-day surroundings, while it at the same time leaves the splendors of the sermon's heights still ringing through their consciousness, to be afterwards recalled at leisure and in quiet (who shall say when or how often throughout the years to come, or indeed while life lasts?). Sometimes, on the very crest of the climax, he abruptly ends with a quick prayer to the All-Father, which of itself inextricably *clinches* in his hearer's heart the sermon's benign invasion.

Reference has been made, in a previous chapter, to his never writing *down* to the level of his readers. In

addresses composed for delivery before students, theological or other,
niggardliness of learning would not
perhaps be expected: but in the
Sermons, addressed to miscellaneous
audiences, the case is not far from
being as bad. His feeling in the
matter would seem to be, it is best to
give — only *give :* if each one does
not grasp it *all*, he will *some :* and
the *attempt* to grasp — the attitude of
reaching *up* — the effort to compre-
hend what one has not as yet thoroughly mastered — is of itself helpful
(much preferable to the supine and
indolent mental posture of one who
is quite on the level of, or even a
little above, what he reads). It is very
noticeable in him that, whether writ-

ing or speaking, he never seems satisfied till the note struck is the *octave-
note*—that view of the matter in hand
which is the *highest* his thought and
life have yielded him — and every subject he handles he seeks to lead up and
attach to the loftiest he knows : he is
never willing to rest till he has
reached that theme. A loyal knight,
ever alert to duty. Dr. Lyman Abbott
has recently remarked of him that
he always *preaches :* any of his after-
dinner speeches he might use the
next Sunday in his pulpit.

Not only is he complex, and instead
of coming down to his readers invites
them to come up to him : he is never
afraid of giving full measure, heaped
up and running over. Into every

address or chapter he puts material enough to make, if more thriftily spread out, four highly respectable ones. Every page scintillates with gems, not only gathered from widely-distant quarters of thought and of feeling, but packed into the smallest space. A discourse of his is like the "dark rich cloth bursting out into jewels from within," which serves him as an illustration in one of his sermons. He may be said to compose *royally*, as who has the storehouse of the Universe and of Eternity behind him, and nothing is further from his thoughts than an intellectual economy. Indeed, his resources and the activity of his brain are such, that it is probably *easier* for him to lavish than to withhold **and** dilute.

It must be confessed, he knows how to feel his way to the deep places of the human heart led by an instinct infallible, and upon the corrupt and sore spots of the soul he lays the renovating and healing touch of a master. Carlyle, speaking of what used to be called " billowy Chalmerian prose," says that " no preacher ever went so into one's heart " as Dr. Chalmers — but when did Carlyle ever state an opinion moderately? In one of the Yale Lectures, if the writer remembers the place correctly, Brooks points out to his hearers, young men preparing for the Christian

ministry (and, through them, to
students of religion at large), how
wondrous and confirming, to the
young priest who goes from his
school out into life, is the revelation of finding that, the longer he
lives, and the deeper he sees into
the surrounding mystery of things,
the more are the teachings of the
Master and of the wise ones, which
he studied during his years of preparation and accepted largely on
trust, corroborated by the world,
the more are they discovered to be
applicable in the way of alleviation
to the world.   This revelation has
clearly been made to him, —and he
is moreover to be credited with
noticeable *originality* of insight and

of application. The " Lectures on Tolerance," for instance — mere suggestion, instead of the elaborate work on the subject that would have been so welcome, and he would have written so well, though they are — are of marked originality. Such production as this it is, that causes Dr. Abbott to indulge in the shrewd conjecture that Phillips Brooks thinks even more than he studies — adding that he entertains the suspicion that he prays. In no sermons recalled by the writer at this moment, are there in proportion to the whole a larger number that, once read, stamp themselves ineffaceably and forever upon the memory and heart, and are found to come up, throughout life — like some of Robertson's, and one or two of the late Dr. George Putnam's — alike in our hours of revery and of crisis, as it were, "with healing on their wings." It seems hardly too much to say that, in the bitterest adversity or affliction, he who has ever read the sermon on the "Consolations of God" will have had done for him the utmost that human means afford.

His style is fitted for and at once suggests his delivery: the same abrupt start, quick getting under headway, and sustained and out-pouring rush. It is like a high-bred racer: there is so much vitality in it, its speed cannot be kept down. Indeed, whenever you take up an address of which you do not know though you may begin to suspect the author, as soon as beneath the growing statement you hear the *gathering rush* you may feel sure you are reading Phillips Brooks. The only prose of his the writer remembers that lacks this decisive trait is the "Memorial History" chapter already referred to —without the signature it would never be known as his. Whatever he writes is written to be spoken. He has the extemporaneous instinct. The main thought or feeling he wishes to express is jumped at at once, and struck out first, leaving the details to fall into place afterwards. As Porson said of Charles James Fox, "he throws himself into the middle of his sentences, and leaves it to Almighty God to get him out again." He often *feels* several times for the exact word he wants, just as one does in speaking, though each time his word of tentation is almost a blow. Nor does he make any extensive experiments in the way of variety of manner. Lowell, to take a single instance, exhibited several quite distinct styles or veins, but Brooks is always Brooks — the same unchanged instantly-recognizable quality wherever met with. It is as if, having in the first place carefully studied a thing and learned to do it well, he had never cared to bother with excursions after universality of form, but just

HOLY TRINITY, PHILADELPHIA.

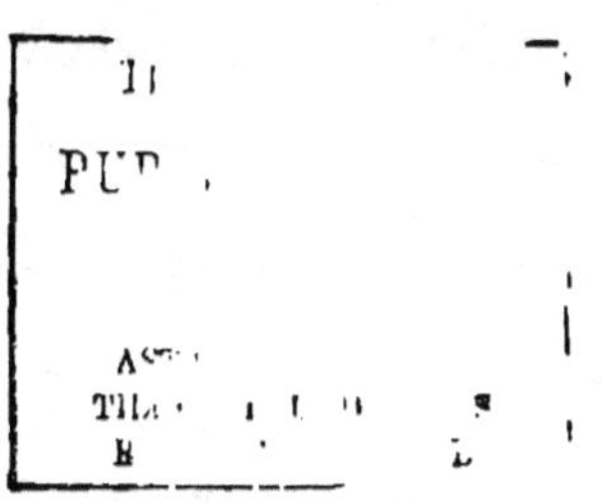

goes on *doing the thing* over and over again.

His vocabulary is copious, pithy and choice. His sentences are short; each sentence and phrase contains its idea rolled into a pellet; each presents a totally new idea, generally drawn from a source widely-different from the last. They follow each other in almost breathless succession. till all the marvelous complexity of the subject he is presenting has been built and welded together and driven home.

WHAT HE STANDS FOR IN THE EPISCOPAL CHURCH.

V.

WHAT HE STANDS FOR TODAY.

IS it asked, what does Phillips Brooks stand for today in the "Protestant Episcopal Church in the United States of America"?

It may be answered : Phillips Brooks in *any* church stands first and foremost for the Fatherhood of God — the sonship of Christ and of man — the inspiration of the Spirit. If we, in the words of Archdeacon Farrar, when speaking of him, " want to know something of

Christianity as Christ taught it, before it was corrupted," we may turn to him.

He believes, above all things, as regards both the Founder and the preachers of Christianity, in personality; in life rather than doctrine ; in giving "not an argument but a man." He says : "If there has been one change which above all others has altered our modern Christianity from what the Christian religion was in apostolic times, I think beyond a doubt it must be this, the substitution of a belief in doctrines for loyalty to a person as the essence and the test of Christian life. . . [The gospels] had no creed but Christ. Christ was their creed." " Not from simple brain

to simple brain, as the reasoning of
Euclid comes to its students, but
from total character to total character, comes the New Testament from
God to men." Again : "The king
must go with his counsellors at his
side and his army at his back, or he
makes no conquest. The intellect
must be surrounded by the richness
of the affections and backed by the
power of the will, or it attains no perfect truth." "The method which in-
cludes all other methods must be in
his [the preacher's] own manhood, in
his character, in his being such a
man, and so apprehending truth himself, that truth through him can come
to other men." This comprehension
or intuition of the supremacy of per-

sonality, for instance, it is that forces him, in his address upon " Biography," delivered at Phillips Exeter Academy, to confess that he would rather have written a great biography than any other great book, and that if he were going to be a painter he would by pre-ference paint portraits. Of his own words it has been said that, like the Master's, they themselves "*are* spirit and *are* life."

To him, again, "religion presents itself   . . as an elemental life in which the soul of man comes into very direct and close communion with the soul of God." Everywhere his utterances, his character, and his life are full of this. In the sermon upon the "Knowledge of God," he points out how Christ " knew God. He sent back adoration, trust, exuberant love in answer to the recognized care which was always pouring itself upon him." This is his ideal for man. He impresses it upon the students whom he seeks to help; he inculcates it in his congregations; he unconsciously illustrates it in his career.

Personality first, uttering itself in fullness and perfection of life. Above all is the Father. Be led by the Spirit to Christ, and " hid with Christ in God "— be joined to Him — let His life flow through you, and supply and impel and restrain and guide you: that is the only thing. It renders all else superfluous. After that, indeed, all else follows of itself.

As God is our Father, so are all men our brothers. Nothing human is to be accounted foreign or alien to us. We are to love even infidels and pagans — Buddhists, Mohammedans, and the worshipers of Hellenic Zeus — as well as the Christians of sects other than ours. Around each one of us lie four concentric circles : the nearest encloses the particular church to which he belongs ; the next distant, the whole body of Christians ; the one after that, those who cherish any religious belief whatever ; the last, all mankind, even those with no religion at all. Of these four, the first — the one enclosing the particular church to which a man belongs — "nestles to its centre with a warmth of sympathy which the others do not know:" and there, stated in his own words, lies Phillips Brooks's Churchmanship.

He is, it may be said, in the first place, a son of God *at first hand;* never out of the presence or the thought of his Father; in direct and intimate relation with Him; receiving his inspiration and credentials immediately from His hand : and as he is, so would he have others be. There is no need for the priest to *over-emphasize* himself, his machinery, or his methods. He is not infallible; he is subject to doubt, to error, to growth, the same as any other man, and would do better never to feel hesitation in saying so. To the men and women of his congregation, whom he has so often instructed from the pulpit, he often finds himself in need to come for instruction and help himself. He is here, not to obtrude *himself*, but only to do what he can towards helping his fellow men put and keep themselves in the same direct, original communication with God that he enjoys, and become his brothers indeed. He is simply a window through which the Light may be seen ; merely a door by which men may enter in. That it is his privilege to be : beyond that he may not hope nor ask.

Different sects are necessitated by the very constitution of human nature.

They have always existed, and always will exist. We talk of the "unity of faith," but it never was nor ever will be possible for Christianity to be in all respects a homogeneous unit. One in impulse, one in purity, one in "fullness and perfection of life," indeed, it may be — that is, one at *heart* — but in matters of the head, of opinion, of doctrine, of organization, it must always contain shades of variance. One who has reached the bottom (or top) of things, and is united with God, will recognize others who are in like manner united. He will feel that they may be so united, and yet differ with him in doctrine or denomination ; he will respect and entertain tolerance for their opinions ;

since these are something decided, and so better than mere indifference, he will, up to a certain point, even admire them for holding them, and rejoice that they do so. "The more men you honor the more cisterns you have to draw from." He may argue with them and seek to arouse their reason to accept his views : he will never exclude, or scorn, or seek to coerce them. Beyond a doubt, he may preach in their pulpits (as Phillips Brooks himself has done). Different men will always see different aspects in the same thing When this is a very large and complex and con-stantly-unfolding thing — as in its applications is Christianity — no one body of observers grasps it all. No

PHILLIPS BROOKS WHEN RECTOR OF HOLY TRINITY PHILADELPHIA.

single denomination can appropriate all the truth in Christianity. For those who do not regard it in all its details just as we do, we should *rejoice* that other denominations exist, to which they may resort. Only an aggregation of progressing denominations can hope to represent or master it all.

And yet in essentials and at bottom Christianity may be comprehended in "a few first large truths." "Every truth is necessary to man which is necessary to righteousness, and no truth is necessary to man which is not necessary to righteousness." "There are excrescences upon the faith which puzzle and bewilder men and make them think themselves unbelievers when their hearts are really faithful. Such excrescences must be cast away."

As to the future life, and punishment — "such as God is can punish such as men are for nothing except wickedness : honestly mistaken opinions are not wicked." "Error is not guilt." "Whatever comes to any man in the other life will come because it must come, because nothing else could come to such a man as he is." " Insincerity (whether it profess to hold what we think is false or what we think is true), cant, selfishness, deception of one's self or of other people, cruelty, prejudice,— these are the things with which the Church ought to be a great deal more angry than she is. The anger which she is ready to expend upon a misbeliever ought to be poured out on these."

What Phillips Brooks stands for in the " Protestant Episcopal Church of America " is thus seen to be something at bottom very simple; very broad, catholic, lofty and grand ; and, it must be confessed, it seems very like the Truth.

DEATH.

VI.

DEATH.

THE consecration of Bishop Brooks was an imposing ceremony. On the morning of October 14, 1891, Trinity Church was completely filled by a congregation largely made up of the culture and wealth of Boston. Officials of the nation, State and city lent dignity to the occasion, and the highest dignitaries of the church participated in the exercises. Two of the brothers of the bishop — Rev. Dr. Arthur Brooks and Rev. John C. Brooks, themselves distinguished clergymen — were the presbyters who attended him as he proceeded slowly and impressively from the chapel down the north aisle of the church and up the broad central aisle, and all recognized the beauty and the appropriateness of the association. His place now was a pew in the body of the church, from the pulpit of which for so many years he had poured out the wealth of his eloquence. He was accompanied to his place by the vestry and wardens of Trinity, and a long procession of clergymen in their robes, who marched with measured step to the music of "Holy, holy, holy," and "The Lord of Abraham Praise." Ten minutes were required to reach the chancel.

When the procession reached the altar the attending ushers stepped aside and the bishops took their places at the altar for the preliminary communion service, which was conducted by Bishop Howe of Central Pennsylvania. The responses to the Commandments were sung by a choir of fifty-two voices, composed of present and past members of the choir of Trinity Church, to music by Gounod. The "Gloria Tibi" was by Durham, and the first hymn was "Go Forth, ye Heralds, in My Name," after which several church announcements were read.

From his pew, Phillips Brooks could see the six hundred clergymen who had gathered about the chancel rail to do honor to the occasion, and hear the eloquent words of Right Rev. Henry C. Potter, bishop of New York, who preached the consecration sermon. It was a noble effort, worthy of the occasion and the man. There was a beautiful personal thread of love and friendship running through it, notably when he spoke of the days of their youth together, and when his voice thrilled upward almost to breaking as he said, turning to the subject of his discourse, " I love you through and through."

Then followed the formal presentation of the elected bishop, the reading of the certificate of election and the canonical testimonial, the consent of the standing committee and of the bishops. The promise of conformity was repeated in a very low voice after Bishop Williams. Then came a pause, and Phillips Brooks lifted his face with a quiet and expressive movement, and looking upward, uttered clearly and fervently, " So help me, God." Again was there an accent of emphasis in the first answer to the first question, " Are you persuaded that you are truly called ? " etc. " I am so persuaded," was the answer ; " I am truly persuaded," with a fervent, upward glance.

The litany and suffrage, the music of the anthem, the retirement of Bishop Brooks and his return, wearing the rest of the Episcopal habit in black and white ; the " Veni Creator Spiritus," repeated above him kneeling, and the ordinance of the laying on of hands, with the adjuration to remember to " stir up the grace of God," given him by this imposition of hands, are part of the solemn and impressive ceremonial that will never be forgotten by those whose privilege it was to witness it. The new offertory anthem given during the collection of the missions, the singing of "Sanctus" and the Eucharistic hymn, and the "Gloria in Excelsis," and the recessional "The Son of God," made the strong and fitting musical expression of all that had gone before.

The administration of the communion, the repeating of the Lord's Prayer by the congregation, the benediction pronounced by Bishop Williams, closed a notable service.

George William Curtis, writing in the " Easy Chair" of *Harper's Magazine*, said of it : " It was a memorable event, none exactly like it in the annals of that communion ; a catholic incident, which demonstrated the superficiality of mere sectarianism and denominational difference. The stalwart champion of his faith, who does not think his own drum ecclesiastic to be the only instrument in the orchestra, becomes the bishop of a wider than his titular diocese, a bishop *in partibus* of God-fearing and men-loving fellow-pilgrims."

The newly consecrated bishop at once set about the execution of his duties with all his accustomed enthusiasm and vigor. One of the reasons, indeed, assigned for leaving Trinity had been that the strain upon him in the bishopric would be less, — seeming to show he felt a physical need of sparing himself. But he never administered the episcopal duties with concession to any such need. Indeed — as expressed by an humble official — he appeared to do as bishop all he had done before, and the new work besides. He preached not infrequently a dozen times a week, and the amount of general labor he took upon himself was simply enormous. Bishop Clark remarked, on once seeing the list of his appointments, that "if he died he would be deserving of no sympathy," as no man had a right to spend himself so unstintedly. On the Sunday following his consecration he administered the rite of confirmation in the smallest parish church of his diocese.

In the mysterious Divine Order, his episcopate was destined to last only a year and three months; but in that short time he effected literally wonders in the way of uniting and magnifying the diocese. It was said that "such an outlook, and such unity among the clergy, as opened for the Episcopal Church and ruled its councils had never been known in any Episcopal diocese in the country ; " "there was more life in the Episcopal Church of Massachusetts than at any previous time in its history." Those who had for years been his opponents on doctrinal or ecclesiastical grounds, had but to meet him personally to become his devoted friends and admirers: this not only within his own denomination, but outside of it. The testimony on this point is conclusive. Those who had opposed his election to the bishopric became his adherents. Wherever he went, his presence seemed to be a sun that chased away all black clouds.

He once wrote : " We are too much in the habit of asking, when a new town or city is offered as a possible field for an Episcopal Church, whether there are any Church people there ; as if that name described a special kind or order of humanity to whom alone we were to consider ourselves as sent. The real question ought to be whether there are human creatures in that town. We are sent to the human race."

In that belief he acted. Says Dr. George E. Ellis, the eminent Unitarian: "It is plain to all of us in this community that while in one of such nobleness of soul there was no lack of love and loyalty for the views and vows and duties which he had espoused and to which he had consecrated himself, he overran all the bounds of sympathy and charity in the universal comprehensiveness of his prompting and purpose, not only to recognize with respect every form and type of religious conviction, but to add his own strong helpfulness in speech and influence to the aims and work of all who were apart, and to whom he offered all that they could crave of fellowship."

Says the *Boston Herald,* editorially: "All the clergy and the people of Boston, and all the clergy and people of Massachusetts, had a part in him, and he was their bishop by the grace of God, and accepted as such, quite as truly as he was the titular bishop of the Protestant Episcopal Church in Massachusetts."

Says the *Boston Transcript,* editorially: " Every man, woman, and child in Massachusetts felt as if they had some part or lot in the work and career of this man."

He was called " our bishop " by members of all denominations, and even by some perhaps who were members of none.

After seeing him administer confirmation, an observer wrote: —

" What was there in his manner, his tone, his soul-utterance, that caused every one to be held spellbound, following him as he bent down in benediction, and as he raised his noble face to heaven to plead that the Good Shepherd keep this member of the flock in the fold? I have seen the ceremony hundreds of times, but never in its completeness before. It was like hearing 'Way Down upon de Suanee River,' sung by Christine Nillson, instead of by incomplete talent, or 'Home, Sweet Home' by Adelina Patti. I was not the only one affected. The scene comes to me as vividly as then — the hushed held-breath absorption of the congregation in the bishop behind the rail, and he, unconscious as it were of them, but actively doing his Master's work, doing it as I had never seen it done before. Was I wrong? I asked those in my company as we walked away if they had been similarly influenced. We were Episcopalians, but not of the Trinity congregation ; and I found the four of us were of one mind. It was a never-to-be-forgotten scene. I have seen great sights in my life. I have seen all England welcoming the young Danish princess to her English home ; the return of the Guards from the Crimea. The great heart of the people throbbed on these occasions as I have never seen it since. I saw Napoleon and Paris welcome his African troops on their return from the desert fields of battle ; I have seen Grant, Sherman, and Blaine welcomed; I have witnessed the thrilling effect of war standards, with strips of the national colors still clinging to them, carried in the streets crowded with people; I have heard the noble Wendell Phillips electrifying an audience in his greatest oration in the Old South; I have heard the polished, gracious Devens, the sarcastic Ingalls, the irony of Conkling, the polish of Sumner, the home-touch of Dickens, the high breeding of Lowell, and the wit of genial Holmes — but what are these in memory to the touch of the divine I witnessed in the little church that Sabbath eve when·the spirit of Easter was abroad and the typical lily symbolized the season!"

The summer before his death he visited England again, preaching in Westminster Abbey, and creating throughout the kingdom a more profound impression than ever he had done before. It was his first visit to England as bishop.

On the fourteenth day of January, 1893, Bishop Brooks caught cold while officiating at the consecration of a church in East Boston, and complained of sore throat. Five days later, Thursday, the 19th, he took to his bed, from which he never again arose. His physician, who was at once summoned, did not consider the case serious, though he ordered great care and extreme quiet for the patient, and had him placed in care of a nurse. The physician was constant in his attendance during Friday and Saturday, but saw no alarming symptoms until late Sunday night. He then called in a brother practitioner, the case having assumed a diphtheritic character. A consultation was held at three o'clock Monday morning, but even at that hour no sign of immediate danger was detected. Soon after the bishop became delirious, and then was attacked with a slight spasm. Immediately following the convulsion the patient's heart grew weaker, and at exactly 6.30 o'clock the bishop ceased to breathe. His last words were spoken to his brother, and were in the nature of a farewell.

Beside the bishop's bedside when the end came were the physicians, the nurse, the bishop's brother William, and the family servants.

It may be said here that Bishop Brooks had known, and some of his intimate friends had known, on competent medical authority, for upwards of ten years, that his death was likely to occur suddenly at any time. During the last five years of his life he had largely lost his ample covering of flesh, and grown very noticeably spare and even gaunt.

It was a subject of frequent remark amongst his friends and acquaintances, that he seemed to be aging more rapidly than is usual at his time of life. When he came home from delivering the sermons at Trinity Church, New York, three years before, he was perceptibly older, and during the last year of his life his hair had grown quite white. The evidence all seemed to show that the diagnosis of the physician, more than ten years before, had been correct; and when the end came it came because, while the attacking disease was in itself slight, the internal powers of resistance were gone. Doubtless, too, the rate at which he worked was hurtful to him from a physical point of view.

The news of this disastrous removal carried consternation throughout the community, and could with difficulty at first be believed. It was like a thunderbolt out of a clear sky. It seemed impossible that such an apparently all-round impregnable tower of strength could have been brought low, as it were, in a moment, without a word of warning. Men stared at the newspaper bulletin boards and refused to credit the evidence of their senses. Ladies poured into the stores as they began to display in their windows draped pictures of the departed, and inquired what it all meant, thinking there was some mistake.

Wherever one stood or passed in the streets one heard the beloved and venerated name on men's lips. Laborers and teamsters called out the sad news to one another. Poor women wept at their work, and even business men did not attempt to hide the tears glistening in their eyes.

The telegraph and telephone did their work. The tidings spread far and wide, and soon from all over the country arose the note of regret and lamentation, coupled with eulogy.

Said the *Nation:* " The death of Phillips Brooks strikes down the greatest figure left to the American church. He long ago rose above his own denomination, and made his large personality a part of broad and progressive Christianity everywhere. Men felt that the fact of his being an Episcopalian was a mere accident, and that his generous nature would have made its own sect, or, rather, absence of all sect, wherever he had found himself placed. Indeed, one may go further, and, echoing Sumner's cry that he was a man before he was a commissioner, say that Phillips Brooks was a man before he was a clergyman. Certainly he could never have been the clergyman he was had he not been the man he was. . . . What he had been as rector, preacher, lecturer, he continued

Old Trinity Church Summer Street, Boston.

to be as bishop — a lover of truth and simplicity, a hater of shams and conventions. His personality and his fame will doubtless remain unique in the history of American Christianity."

Said the New York *Evening Post:* " Never perhaps has the religious world in the United States suffered so severe and crushing a blow as that which has been dealt it by the death of Phillips Brooks, who, by reason of his moral health and strength, his intellectual culture, his splendid powers as an orator, his high courage, his personal charm and comprehensive liberality of thought and act, was a noble representative of the highest type of the modern churchman. . . . One man like Bishop Brooks fills tens of thousands of the younger generation with the noble discontent which alone keeps the public conscience alive."

Said Chauncey M. Depew : "The death of Phillips Brooks is a national calamity. The world is smaller and poorer by his departure. He filled a great place in connection with the intellectual development of the country upon religious lines. He accomplished the most difficult feat of any churchman in this country, and, I think, abroad. He was placed in the midst of the highly cultivated and brilliant Unitarianism of

Boston, and substantially captured it. He was almost the only churchman whose death will be regretted by people of all other sects. The principles, the practice, and the superb expression of his theology and his humanity, brought him very near to the heart of the great mass of the American people."

Said Joseph Cook: "New England has waited a century for a man of his magnificent depth of character, and we are all personally bereaved. A part of my life is buried in his grave. Some could have wished that his attitude toward certain reforms could have been more pronounced. But his influence was wholesome and precious. When we remember that his sphere of activity was national and international, we shall regard that his loss will be felt in England as well as in New England. He represented manly, progressive Christianity."

Said Edward Everett Hale: "Too broad for sect, too large for party, and too wise for controversy, he accepted every opportunity in the service of his Master, by which he could elevate the people to the highest and noblest life. He was too brave to shrink from any duty, as he was too humble to refuse any. His matchless power of speech was the fit result of the purity of his life and the manliness of his purpose. And in his sympathy with all, young and old, high and low, he carried everywhere the gospel which he loved, so as to make it command the attention of all who saw him, or heard him, or knew him. There is no one left who had so many friends."

Said Edwin D. Mead: "As we think of his great and divine life to-day, which we here in Boston have chiefly been privileged to see and touch, who can fail to feel, as the men of Florence felt who heard and knew Savonarola, that every poor and miserable image which we treasure — the poor political ambition, the paltry love of money and the things that money buys, the indulgences of culture, the literary vanities, the social jealousies, the resentments that sterilize, the sorrow that consumes, each thing that is not pure and universal — should be hurried to the square and burned, as an expression of that devotion and high resolve to have here a better city, a loftier public and personal life, which is the only expression of gratitude which he ever cared for or cares for. Phillips Brooks's influence upon our general American religious life and thought cannot to-day be estimated. Too religious, too reverent and too great for controversy, he has gone on conquering place for his deep, broad, and catholic thought in his own church and in all churches simply by his positive, synthetic preaching of it, and by living it and being it. He was a man greater than all churches — the friend and fellow of all who live in the spirit. Whatever his own cherished theological doctrines and whatever his own chosen and dear ecclesiastical relations, his church was nothing less than the Church of the Living God, the church of all just and generous and loving men."

Said one who knew him at Oxford, England: "There are many in England who will mourn the death of Bishop Brooks — mourn not merely a mighty preacher, a magnificent man, but a true friend. More than any man I have ever known, Phillips Brooks possessed that which commanded instant trust, complete confidence, — a power not only the outcome of a splendid physique, eloquent of strength and protection, of a broad, quick, and ever sympathetic mind, but of a great heart filled with love for all his fellow-beings, a love blind to all differences of class and of race, and which shone ever from his kindly eyes, lit up his face with a sunny smile, and made him godlike."

His funeral occurred on Thursday,

January 26, and was a public one. The following description of it is taken from the columns of the daily press : —

If any testimony were needed of the affection of the people of Boston for Phillips Brooks, it was afforded on that day by the great crowd that assembled about Trinity Church at an early hour, and continued to gather until the last opportunity for gazing upon his beloved face had gone by. Beginning with the little group that appeared in Copley Square before 7.30 o'clock, it continued to increase until at one time there was a line of people extending from there to Berkeley Street, almost making the sidewalk impassable. Indeed, it would have been so but for the services of a large body of police, who kept the people so compact as to afford a narrow passageway. At 7.45 the coffin enclosing the remains was borne from the bishop's residence at the corner of Clarendon and Newbury Streets, accompanied by a guard of the Loyal Legion, of which organization Bishop Brooks was chaplain. It was taken to the church and placed in the vestibule, the centre of which was shrouded in the heaviest black. The coffin was covered with the colors of the Loyal Legion, upon which lay a cluster of Easter lilies, intermingled with palms.

The plate bore this inscription:

PHILLIPS BROOKS,
BISHOP OF THE DIOCESE OF MASSACHUSETTS.
December 13, 1835.
January 23, 1893.

Details from the Loyal Legion did duty as guards of honor, relieving each other every hour.

Fully three hundred people were in line when the doors were opened at eight o'clock, and from that time on there was an uninterrupted procession of people, divided into two files after entering the doors, one passing on one side of the coffin and the other on the opposite, uniting again at the south door, through which they passed on to St. James Avenue. A view of the bishop's face was obtained through a heavy plate of glass, hermetically sealed.

The people who were thus afforded a view of a face grand and impressive even in death, were of all conditions of life. Gentlemen and ladies in rich and elegant attire walked side by side with persons wretchedly dressed and bearing all the evidence of severe poverty. Large numbers of children, evidently from poor and humble homes, waited patiently and decorously in the long line for an opportunity to see one whom they remembered as having said kindly words of cheer to them when he had visited the homes of their parents or addressed them in their Sunday schools. When the doors were closed, soon after eleven o'clock, thousands were yet in line and lingered about the square for the brief service which was to be said in their presence.

At all the other entrances there were large gatherings of people who had reason to suppose that a place would be found for them inside the church. It was a difficult task to keep them in order and discriminate as to their claims for precedence.

It is estimated that fully twelve thousand people viewed the remains of Bishop Brooks as they lay in state. For the first hour the people had filed by at the rate of sixty a minute. Then it increased to eighty a minute. Among them was an old woman, shabbily dressed. with gray hair and careworn face, who, when she reached the casket, drew a beautiful cluster of roses from her bosom and placed it upon the casket. When she turned away her tears were streaming down her cheeks. One Chinaman was amongst the number.

A woman with wan face and the scantiest raiment, whose every appearance indicated a life of penury, stood shivering in the crowd. Tugging at her dress was a little boy, who, like his mother, showed traces of want and suffering, his clothing being thin and insufficient, and even his shoes being so worn as to afford him little protection. The woman, as the crowd surged about the doors, gently touched the arm of a policeman, and begged to be allowed to enter the church. The officer, noticing her humble appearance, roughly brushed her aside, telling her to get into line. "Oh, but I must see him once more; he paid for the operation which gave sight to my boy, and I must see him again."

This came in pleading tones, and she grasped the hand of her little boy all the more tightly, while the tears ran down her cheeks. Her words went straight to the heart of every one within hearing. An usher quietly stepped forward, told the officer to allow the woman to enter, and mother and boy, in their poor, humble way, paid their last tribute to him whose heart and hand and purse had been used to open the world to the view of the little blind boy.

While the host was passing through the vestibule where the bishop's body lay, the delegations were fast filing in through the St. James-Avenue and Clarendon-Street doors. By 11.30 all the pews were taken, and many were stand-

ing in the choir-gallery and in the aisles.
About this time the professors and students of the Episcopal School of Massachusetts, at Cambridge, entered, attired in their black surplices, and took their places on the right of the broad aisle. Soon after the rectors of the Massachusetts diocese, attired in their white surplices, entered and took seats opposite the students, the congregation standing as they filed in. They were followed by a number of rectors from other dioceses, who took seats in the chancel.

The entire north (or left) side of the floor and the north gallery were reserved for the congregation of Trinity Parish, who entered at the Clarendon-Street entrance.

Pews on the middle aisle were reserved for the clergy who could not be provided for in the chancel, visiting clergy from other dioceses, the immediate family, standing committee of the diocese, honorary pall-bearers, the wardens and vestry of Trinity Church, the Governor and committee of the Legislature, Mayor of Boston, President of Harvard College and the corporation, members of the Harvard class of 1855, delegation from the Massachusetts Commandery of the Loyal Legion, and personal friends. The entire south side of the church, both floor and gallery, was reserved for the diocesan organizations, the officers and students of the Episcopal Theological School, delegations from St. Mark's School and Groton School, the Board of Missions, directors and lay missionaries of the Episcopal City Mission, general officers of the Massachusetts Women's Auxiliary, trustees of donations, directors of Church Home for Orphans and Destitute Children, managers of the Girls' Friendly Society, St. Luke's Home for Convalescents, Episcopal Church Association, Episcopalian Club, officers of Young Men's Christian Union, representatives of Young Men's Christian Association, Trinity Club, Boston University.

The funeral arrangements were beautifully carried out with the aid of a large corps of marshals. These marshals were the same gentlemen who had officiated at Bishop Brooks's consecration less than two years before.

There were many clergymen present representing many denominations.

It was much like Easter Day in the church, for although there were the deep draperies of mourning, there was also the same display of flowers one sees at the festival that marks the close of Lent. The great cross of lilies in the chancel, the lilies upon the coffin of the dead bishop, and almost the first sweet, springlike sunshine that had come during that cold January, all together seemed to impress the feeling of the day of resurrection upon the thousands of assembled people.

The interior of the church, including the chancel, walls and railing, pulpit, reading-desk and gallery, was all heavily draped, and in beautiful relief the chancel itself was decorated with floral and other appropriate emblems. At the back of the chancel was an arch of laurel fifteen feet high and nine feet in width, flanked on each side by two spruce-trees eight feet in height. Directly in front of this arch, on a sort of dais, rested a tall and beautiful cross of Easter lilies, and at the side was the baptismal font concealed by laurel and filled with Easter lilies. The chancel railing was wound with laurel, and upon it, in a row, were small potted spruce-trees. The artistic effect was of a pyramid, and the trees were so tapered as to conform to that idea.

During the morning hours boxes of flowers were arriving from the florists, principally roses and lilies, and were piled up in the open space before the altar. After ten o'clock no attempt was made at arranging them, and they were simply massed wherever a suitable place could be found for them.

Just before noon the doors opened from the vestibule and the funeral procession entered, headed by Rev. Dr. Donald, rector of Trinity, and followed by the six bishops — Bishop Williams of Connecticut, Bishop Niles of New Hampshire, Bishop Neely of Maine, Bishop Clark of Rhode Island, Bishop Randolph of Virginia, and Bishop Talbot of Wyoming. The eight members of the standing committee of Trinity Church came next, and behind them the bier, borne on the shoulders of eight men picked from the various athletic teams of Harvard College. The twelve honorary bearers followed : Dr. W. N. McVickar of Philadelphia, Justice Gray of the United States Supreme Court, Rev. Percy Browne, Hon. Robert C. Winthrop, Dr. C. A. L. Richards of Providence, President Eliot of Harvard College, Rev. Leighton Parks of Emmanuel Church, Colonel Charles Russell Codman, Rev. Professor A. V. S. Allen, Robert Treat Paine, C. T. Morrill, and Dr. H. Weir Mitchell of Philadelphia. The family and the wardens and vestrymen of Trinity Church brought up the rear.

The body was placed at the head of the broad aisle just outside the chancel.

After the silence of the moment following the placing of the coffin, the

burial service began. The voice of
Bishop Potter shook while he read the
opening lines of the two hymns which
were sung by all the congregation,
" Jesus, lover of my soul," and " For all
the saints who from their labors rest,"
led by the old quartet ; but during the
service it was clear and firm, and at times
almost triumphant in quality, particularly in the reading, " There is one glory
of the sun, and another glory of the
moon, and another glory of the stars ;
for one star differeth from another star
in glory. So also is the resurrection of
the dead. It is sown in corruption ; it
is raised in incorruption ; it is sown in
dishonor ; it is raised in glory."

There was no eulogy, of course.
Only the violets of mourning spoke
to the people from the black-hung pulpit. After the last prayer and the
benediction of grace, the coffin was
carried again down the broad aisle, and
during the service outside everybody
remained standing while the low notes
of the organ and the sound of sobbing
made the silence of the church seem
deeper.

No one in that vast throng of people
which had assembled in Copley Square
at noon can ever forget the scene.
From an early hour the crowd had been
gathering, and as it passed through the

vestibule where the body of Bishop Brooks lay in state, many still lingered about for the service which had been announced after that in the church. A hollow square was roped off about the centre doors, and within it was a solid row of policemen. Every inch of space on the immense steps, the sidewalk, and the surrounding streets was packed with hundreds of men and women, representing every walk of life. That it was no crowd of curious idlers, a hasty look would show, but sincere mourners, who showed by their presence their intense longing to pay some tribute of respect to him who was the loyal friend of all classes. Many found it impossible to get near the church, and they filled the steps of the Art Museum and all of the neighboring buildings, while from the private houses of the immediate vicinity other interested spectators looked upon the extraordinary scene from wide-opened windows. At half-past twelve the great doors swung back, and the heavily draped coffin was brought into the sunlight and placed on the elevated frame, which was also draped.

Rev. Dr. Donald took his position at the left, with the pallbearers grouped about. The short, impressive prayer was delivered by the rector in a clear voice, while profound silence fell upon

BURNING OF OLD TRINITY CHURCH, BOSTON

the listening multitude. As he closed his book and stretched his hands toward the crowd, saying, "Let us all join in the Lord's Prayer," every head was bowed and every lip seemed to move in prayer.

It was a thrilling scene. Strong men, unused to any show of feeling, felt no shame at the big tears that splashed down their faces, and the only other sound besides the murmur of hushed voices was an occasional sob.

The assistant rector then read the hymn beginning, —

> "O God, our help in ages past,
>   Our hope for years to come,
> Our shelter from the stormy blast,
>   And our eternal home,"

copies of which were distributed among the crowd. Three cornetists stood at the left of the officiating clergyman, and led the singing.

Dr. Donald then pronounced a benediction, and the mourners came from the church to the carriages which very in waiting, and the crowd slowly — very slowly and sadly — dispersed.

The carriages being taken, a procession was formed which proceeded to Mount Auburn by way of the Harvard Bridge. Hundreds of people had collected along the line of its progress ; all places of business passed by it were closed; and no person gazed upon it but showed in his demeanor solemnity and respect.

When, coming up Harvard Street, its head reached Beck Hall, Cambridge, a few minutes before two o'clock, the University bell began tolling, and the students gathered in great numbers. They lined up on both sides of the drive from University out to the west gate, standing three deep, with hundreds of the town people who had assembled to witness the impressive demonstration, standing in the rear of the lines. The procession halted at the Main-Street entrance sufficiently long to enable students to get into position; then it slowly passed into the yard. As the carriages filed by, every head was bared, and all remained uncovered until the last vehicle in the procession drove out of the gate. The scene was as picturesque as it was impressive, and what gave additional solemnity to the occasion was the chiming of Pleyel's Hymn from the belfry of Christ Church, and the tolling of the old college bell in Harvard Hall. The college flag was at half-mast. A large number of students followed the procession a short distance on its way to the cemetery.

A funeral assembly of one hundred

or more persons was waiting at the cemetery when the procession arrived. Here the old-fashioned, black iron fence that still conservatively encloses the Brooks family lot was entirely covered with evergreen and flowers. In the centre, the mound formed by the earth thrown from the grave was surmounted by a broken shaft of lilies capped with carnations, white roses, sheaves of wheat, and ferns. The posts of the railing were hung with wreaths of ivy and violets tied with purple ribbon.

In the rear of the lot was a large open book, inscribed "The Light of the World." Near it was a second shaft, encircled with an ivy wreath. There were a number of other wreaths lying about.

In the lot are buried the bishop's father and mother, and his two brothers, Rev. Frederic and George.

On a temporary platform before the lot the burial service was read. Those who had assembled before the funeral procession arrived gathered at the top of the hill in the rear while the procession from the carriages gathered upon the platform. The young body-bearers from Harvard tenderly brought the coffin from the hearse and placed it beside the open grave. The service, which was brief, was read by the bish-

op's two brothers — Rev. John Brooks
and Rev. Arthur Brooks.   At the close
of the service there was a slight sur-
ging toward the lot, and there was
scarcely any one present who did not
bear away with him some memento in
the shape of a flower or a bit of green
that had lain by the grave of their beloved bishop.

From twelve o'clock to two, during
the funeral services, there was a general
suspension of business throughout the
city, even the stock exchange closing
its doors; and the routes of many of the
lines of street cars were changed, in
order not to incommode the people who
desired to congregate in Copley Square.

In the First Baptist Church, across
the way from the home of Bishop Brooks,
a large congregation assembled at a simple service at the same hour when the
funeral was being held at Trinity.

The proposed exercises in the Old
South were given up to allow every one
to be present at the out-door services.

In the Church of the Advent two re-
quiem services were held in memory of
Bishop Brooks, the first a communion
service at 7.30.   At 9.30 o'clock the
rector of the church was the celebrant
at a full choral service.   The church
was filled.

A special service was held in memory of Bishop Brooks in St. Augustine's Protestant Episcopal Church, Phillips Street, West End.

Special memorial services were held at different times by the Boston Young Men's Christian Association and Young Men's Christian Union, by "clergymen of all denominations" in the Old South Meeting House, at Appleton Chapel, Harvard College, in the Chapel of Boston University, and in the churches or halls of various cities and towns throughout New England and outside of it. In the service at the Old South Meeting House both Catholics and Protestants united, for the first time in the history of Boston. Bishop Potter, of New York, who had preached the sermon at the episcopal consecration, had intended to preach a memorial sermon in Trinity Church, Boston, on the Sunday following the funeral, but was prevented by illness. Organizations, societies and clubs of all kinds and denominations all over the country held commemorative meetings, or passed resolutions, and the list of meetings — business or convivial — that were adjourned out of respect to the memory of the great dead would be a long one. All Episcopal churches throughout the diocese removed their Christmas decorations, and replaced them with mourning drapings. The colored people of Boston passed resolutions.

At the memorial service celebrated at Appleton Chapel, Harvard University, Professor F. G. Peabody during his address said : —

"The life of a great man has two sides. First, there is the public side, the official recognized life, the power, the eloquence ; and then there is the private side, the personal, the intimate life.

" Sometimes the knowledge of a man's private life does not bring with it an increase of love, but when knowledge of the inner life brings more love with it, then we forget the greatness of the man in the thoughts of his graciousness.

" It is our peculiar privilege here, while the world is honoring the public life of a great man, to honor his private life.

" He came to us not as an orator, but as a brother, a father, a helper. He brought us all his spiritual gifts and a beautiful tenderness and simpleness, as though he found himself here in the trusted circle of domestic life.

.   .   .   .

" In the little book we have in which our preachers record their impressions, there are many observations in his handwriting about the privilege he felt he had in coming here.

"In this chapel to-day there are many men who talked with him, perhaps only once or twice, but they feel they have lost a friend. As some of them have said, they went to him afraid of his greatness, and came away impressed with his kindness."

A popular subscription was at once started for the purpose of erecting a statue to him in Copley Square, in front of the Trinity Church which he had loved so deeply and served **so well.**

BROOKSIANA.

VII.

BROOKSIANA.

BISHOP BROOKS, always an exceedingly hard-working man, after his ascendancy to the bishopric, had his energies taxed to their utmost capacity. He was never, however, known to acknowledge that he needed rest. His duties as bishop of the diocese of Massachusetts were but a small part of his work. Not a day passed but letters and invitations asking his attendance at banquets, clubs, and other social functions were received, and it was his invariable rule to accept, if it was possible for him to do so. Every letter of whatever nature received by him was scrupulously answered, a private secretary being required after he had assumed the bishopric to attend to his correspondence. He never used postal-cards for any purpose. Letters came to him on all subjects from all parts of the world.

Once while abroad he received a letter from a woman in the South who desired to move to Boston with her two children. She wrote to ask the bishop if he would find some nice, moderately-priced boarding-house for herself and family. The bishop sent it back to his secretary, asking him to make inquiries and forward her the desired information. " Be sure," wrote Bishop Brooks, " and tell her that the answer was not delayed any longer than absolutely necessary. Explain to her that I am in Europe." This woman probably never knew the amount of trouble she had caused the bishop and his secretary by her one simple request.

Soon after he was consecrated, the bishop received a letter from a widow in Minnesota. She had been married in Massachusetts and her husband had been killed in the civil war. As a soldier's widow she was entitled to a pension from the government, but this she was unable to obtain, although none disputed the fact of the husband being killed in an engagement and while fighting nobly. But the poor afflicted widow could not prove that this man was her husband, as she had lost her certificate. So she wrote to Bishop Brooks, telling him of her condition and the necessity of receiving a copy of her marriage certificate. She only knew the name of the minister who had married her, and he had died. The bishop of Massachusetts took a personal interest in her case, and worked hard to obtain evidence of the marriage, and was finally successful, and she got her pension.

Then a man down in some Southern State wrote to him to say that he had got to go to New York to get a difficult surgical operation performed, and had no money. He wanted help. The bishop told his secretary to write to the clergyman in his town to inquire about it, and say that if it was all right he would pay it.

Then a man wrote to him to know if he could help him get a certificate of his baptism. All he could tell was that he was baptized in a high church in Montreal. The bishop showed it to his secretary and asked if he could do anything for him; and he sent the applicant a list of all the churches in Montreal and the rectors of each one, that he might write to them.

Fond mothers (and they were not confined to the Episcopalian fold) whose sons were leaving home to make for themselves a place and a name in the busy city, wrote to Bishop Brooks and asked him to keep an eye on their boys, little knowing what a multitude of cares rested upon his broad and massive shoulders.   And so on with many other cases.

A friend who knew Bishop Brooks quite well entered his study one forenoon.   Before the great preacher lay a heap of opened letters.   Turning in his chair he said, "Among all those letters which I have answered, or shall answer, not one appertains to my parish.   All are from people outside the bounds of Trinity, and most of them from people outside of Boston.   They are on all sorts of subjects, and several contain urgent appeals for money."

He was very free with his money, although he never wasted a cent, and was continually doing good deeds with it. He did them quietly, and it was seldom that any one ever heard of it.   He was always thoughtful of his brothers in the ministry, and his sympathies for poor clergymen were especially tender.   On one occasion he received a check for a hundred dollars from a parish in whose church he had preached.   When the check came back to the drawer through the bank it bore the indorsement of a poor clergyman in another part of the State to whom he had sent it.   No one ever knew of it except by that indorsement on the check, which told the story of his generosity.

An Episcopal chapel had been built

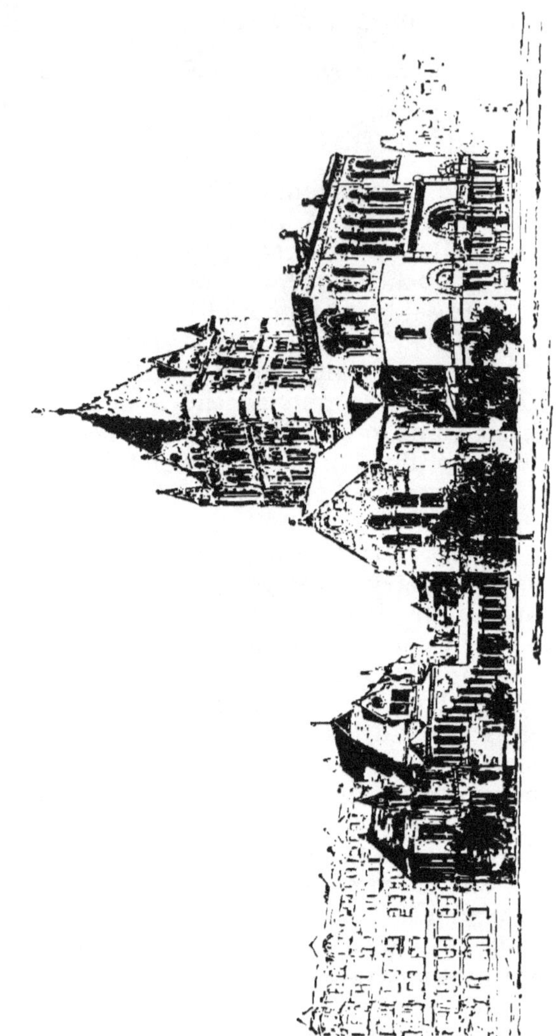

TRINITY CHURCH, BOSTON — EXTERIOR

in one of the remoter suburban towns, and the debt upon it was a heavy burden. Some jesting layman, talking the matter over with Mr. Brooks — both having a little personal interest in the village — said to Trinity's pastor, " I will give as much as you will give toward the extinction of that debt." — " Very well," replied Mr. Brooks, " I will give five hundred dollars." And the debt was paid.

Another incident in the great preacher's life was mentioned as having taken place during a convention held in Baltimore. Dr. Brooks had been invited to preach a missionary sermon in one of the churches. He consented, and the fact being advertised beforehand, the church was so crowded that it was impossible to take up the collection. Hearing of this, Bishop Brooks went to the rector after the people had gone and said, " Well, my dear fellow, I am sorry to have spoiled your collection, but if you can give me an estimate of about the amount you would have had, I will let you have my check for it."

The young candidates for the clergy were his especial pride, and in their progress he had an active personal interest. He helped them pecuniarily, had them visit him, and corresponded with them. He helped many a needy young man through college. He said once to a friend during one of the very few times when he said anything, however personal, in any way connected with his good works : " When you spend a night at a clergyman's house you can generally find out a great deal." This was a very pregnant remark, and it intimated a great line of his charity.

It was his custom in making his visitations to notice the various little things needed in the homes of the poorer clergymen where he was being entertained. He generally did find out a great deal, and what he found out he remembered. As a result, the poor churchman generally received just what he had needed and had been unable to get, and at the hands of the bishop.

About two years ago a printer employed on one of the Boston daily papers fell sick. A subscription was raised among the men in his office to help him make a trip to California. One day the cashier in the counting-room called up through the speaking-tube to the foreman of the composing-room and said, —

" A gentleman wishes to see you."

"All right ; send him up. I would go down, but I can't leave my work."

In a few minutes the foreman was astonished to see the familiar face and form of Boston's great preacher entering the composing-room, four flights from the street, and there is no elevator there. Bishop Brooks said he had learned of what the printers were doing for one of their fellow-workmen, and made some inquiries as to the character of the man. He said this man's wife had attended his church, and he had learned of their misfortunes. Satisfied that it would be a kind act to a worthy man, Bishop Brooks quietly slipped a twenty-dollar note into the foreman's hand, and asked him to add that to the fund, refusing to allow his name to be added to the subscription list.

His work among the poor and lowly was greater than one would dream of. People who had never entered his church, some of whom had never heard him preach, did not fear to ask him to officiate when death invaded the family circle, and they rarely asked in vain. He never refused if he had time at his disposal to grant the request. Once a gentleman who had met him, but who was not his parishioner and not a member of the Episcopal Church, lost his little child. The father and mother wished to have the great preacher, the tender, loving shepherd of the flock, read the burial service over the body of the child. Mr. Brooks said, "I will do so, cheerfully, if I have time." He consulted his list of engagements for the day. "I have just half an hour that is not bespoken ; if you will make your arrangements conform to that time, I will gladly be present."

A physician tells a story of a poor woman who had required his services and to whom he had said, after several visits, "You don't need any more medicine. What you need now is nourishment and fresh air. You need to get out." — "But I have nobody to leave with the children," she said. They were little ones, and the poor mother's anxiety about them had added to her illness. The doctor repeated, "Well, you must manage to get out, somehow." A day or two later — being a sympathetic soul — he dropped in to see if she had found means to obey his directions. She certainly had. She had told her need to the man who cheerfully met all sorts of demands upon him. He was there taking care of the children while the poor mother went out for air and exercise. It was Phillips Brooks!

A visitor to the house in Clarendon Street waited in the hall one day while Bishop Brooks finished a little talk he was having with a workman in the library. He went to the door with this visitor, a middle-aged man, who wore a look of relief as if he had just had a burden taken off his mind. The bishop was saying, "Yes ; that will be your best way," and repeated some advice about the man's work and wages, evidently clinching advice already given. The man hesitated a minute, while the bishop's hand was on the knob, then said, getting his hand towards his pocket, "Shall I — that is, how much would it be ? " with an evident feeling that there ought to be some sort of fee. And the bishop said, "Nothing at all — nothing at all," so heartily and cheerily that the man could not possibly have felt, even after going away, that he had made a mistake in offering to fee Bishop Brooks !

In the broad field of labor through which Bishop Brooks's interests were distributed, very near to his heart was undoubtedly the work of St. Andrew's Church on Chambers Street.

This mission was organized about seventeen years ago, and was called the Chapel of the Evangelists. For two years the work was conducted under the direction of Emmanuel parish, and then it came fully under the ministration and care of Trinity. After a few years of progress two fine buildings were erected on Chambers Street, where Bishop Brooks's ideas could be more fully carried out. Not only did he seek the spiritual welfare of the people who came under his attention, but he always strove to solve the industrial problem ; and what has been accomplished there shows how energetic its laborers have been. It was here that the first girls' club in the country was organized, and its members will recall with much pleasure the many happy occasions when Dr. Brooks entertained them with bright talks about his travels in foreign lands. The dispensary work excited his warmest interest, and it was through his energies that it was kept open at night to answer calls from the sick and suffering —the first attempt in this city of a similar nature. Such a work as St. Andrew's has demanded a large outlay of money, and it was through his personal appeals and his own generous and frequent donations that its present success has been attained.

The Vincent Hospital, too, was another branch of Trinity work in which he always manifested an unfailing sympathy. The Guild Hall of St. Andrews is hung with attractive pictures, which were given by Bishop Brooks, and on festival occasions, when the big family was gathered there, it was his great delight to be present and join with the children in their merry-making. All those who have given of their time and service to the carrying on of Trinity's missions can testify to the appreciation of their labors by their beloved pastor.

Two young men who had been attending Trinity Church, but for some reason or other had ceased going, tell this story. They did not suppose they were known to the rector even by sight. They were rooming at the top — in fact, in the attic — of an unusually high lodging-house in a not very aristocratic quarter of the city, when one afternoon came a rap at their chamber door. On opening it, they found Dr. Brooks standing there, with his kindly smile, hand outstretched, and the following words issuing from his lips: "Well, boys, you did not expect to see *me* here, did you?" As usual careless for himself, he had climbed all the long flights, instead of sending for them to come down to him. The talk that ensued made both the wanderers permanent attendants at Trinity.

His attitude in respect to remuneration for his work was best exemplified at the diocesan convention after his election as bishop was consummated. Previous to this not a word had been said as to salary, and Bishop Paddock had been receiving six thousand dollars and a house on Chestnut Street, owned by the diocese.   At the convention ex-Governor Rice moved that the salary be increased to eight thousand dollars, the amount Phillips Brooks received as rector of Trinity.   The bishop at once got a friend of his to object to this, and ask an indefinite postponement of the matter; and in deference to his wishes it was done.

His private secretary once said of him : —

" Bishop Brooks was in the first place, what a number of clergymen did not believe he could be, a great administrator.   He administered the affairs of the diocese in a broad and warm-hearted manner that endeared those to him who were previously opposed.

" He always found time to talk with any one, but never longer than the subject required.   If it was a matter that necessitated a hearing for two or three hours, he would find time for it, but if it was only an invitation to attend some service, a minute sufficed to settle the matter.   The bishop was a man who had a wonderful faculty for getting at the heart of a thing.   You only had to make a few words of explanation, and he had grasped the whole matter with remarkable comprehension.

" The bishop always seemed to have time for everything, although he was a great worker. I consider myself a pretty hard worker, but I could not pretend to accomplish the amount of work Bishop Brooks did, and he never seemed to be too busy, never hurried. He could always bear an interruption. Sometimes I would say, ' Bishop, I would like to talk to you about a matter when you are at leisure.' Looking up he would instantly reply, ' Well, now is the best time.'

" His mind was like one great reservoir, always full and never needing replenishing. Most clergymen have to labor on a sermon, but he never did. Bishop Brooks wrote his sermons without any apparent effort, for his mind was full of great thoughts. He could write a sermon in six hours, at two sittings.

" I recollect just before the first diocesan convention, when I observed that he was not working on his address. As most bishops would wish to have their first address a particularly good one, I asked him one day if he realized how near the time of the convention was. He replied 'yes,' and then I mentioned his address. ' Oh ! that will be all right,' he replied.

" Sure enough, a day or two before the convention he showed me a bound manuscript, which was the convention address. He had completed it by working an hour or so or less at a time on it. It was one of the grandest things I ever heard him deliver, I think.

"People wonder how he stood such a round of Episcopal invitations and so much travelling. The travelling did not seem to tire him. It rested him. The time he spent on railway trains seemed to be a refreshment to him. I remonstrated with him once against the way he was driving himself, and told him he did not have any time to himself. 'Why, yes, I do; plenty of it,' he said, with his cheery smile. 'I should like to know when and where,' I said. 'Why,' he replied, 'on the railway cars.' And that was about all the time he had to himself.

"And yet, hard as he worked, Bishop Brooks was happy. His life was filled with happiness. He loved his work devotedly. It was not work to him, it was his enjoyment.

"He was the most unselfish man I ever knew. He was always sacrificing himself for others. Not only did he never speak of himself, but he never even thought of himself."

He was very careful in keeping any appointments, and absolutely sincere in any expression. The response, "I will do it if I can," from Bishop Brooks did

not mean, " I will do it if, at the time,
I feel inclined," but meant the literal
significance of the words.

He never used the same sermon or
address a second time, no matter how
similar the occasions or in how distantly
separated sections of the country they
might be.

Socially he was the simplest and most
cordial and even jovial of men. Every
man, woman, and child who ever came
in contact with him in any of the multi-
tudinous interests of which he was a living part must always remember how
completely he practised what he preached
of the gospel of sincerity and simplicity
and love. He was a type of the largest,
broadest, most benevolent humanity,
and had the keenest interest in all that
was calculated to uplift. He thought of
the whole human being, and studied
him in all his various phases. He was
easy and agreeable in his manners in
the presence of ladies, but his meanest
enemy — if the good man had one —
would never accuse him of being a
" ladies' man." On the contrary, Bishop
Brooks treated a woman in the same
frank, open manner he would if he were
talking with a man, which was always
gratifying to the intelligent woman, who
was at once placed at her best in his
society.

In connection with Dr. Brooks's celibacy many amusing stories were told, intimating that his bachelorhood was, to say the least, not a matter of necessity. His treatment of all hints and remarks on the subject of the admiration alleged to be heaped upon him by female parishioners and friends in general, showed his innate modesty and avoidance of self-assertion. In tones of comic protestation he would say, "Talk about my being overwhelmed with slippers! Why, often I haven't a pair to put on when I really need them." "Ah, I suppose that's a gift from some admirer, Phillips?" said his brother on one occasion, pointing to a handsome basket of fruit standing on the table. With an air of *nonchalance*, Dr. Brooks pushed the basket before his brother, saying, "They're good, aren't they? Eat them, boy, eat them," and nothing more definite could be got from him.

His love for children was well known. A group of children pleased him more than a group of elders. He could so easily enter into their joys. A child at the Church Home, South Boston, just fresh from reading "Jack, the Giant Killer," looking at his height, accosted him one day with these words, "Be you a giant?" — "Yes, my dear," was the reply. Others would take delight in climbing into his lap, and he would show them some relic from Japan, which he always carried, to their great amusement.

Helen Kellar of the blind school was very dear to him; he loved to talk with her about the Divine Being. After service in a church, if he knew she was there, he would go at once, after disrobing, from the vestry room, and with extended arms most affectionately greet the afflicted girl.

It is believed that a correspondence was kept up between Helen Kellar and Bishop Brooks up to the time of the latter's death. Bishop Brooks's simplicity of faith was never better illustrated than in his beautiful letter to Helen when her alert mind began to consider the questions of the soul and immortality.

It is told of the bishop that one time, at some informal meeting where there were a great many children, he felt a strange sensation about one of his knees — a queer, repeated jabbing sensation. And when it came the third time he realized that it was external, and looked down to see a tiny girl gravely sticking in a pin. "Well, well, little girl, what are you doing?" he exclaimed; and she lisped, "I just wanted to see if you's stuffed!" His great size had impressed her; her inquiring turn of mind proved to be an introduction which greatly amused her new friend, who afterwards did a good deal for the child, whose mother too needed help.

It was at the Christmas sale at Trinity Church. A little girl who had some dolls for sale begged the bishop to buy one from her table. Just to make talk with her, apparently, the bishop asked, "Now, what kind of dolls are you selling?" — " Brides," said the child. The bishop laughed. "Won't you have one?" persisted the little girl. She was too young to know why the bishop laughed so much after her answer to his next question. "Now, what should I do with a bride?" — "Why, you could give her away!"

Said a writer in the *Boston Transcript:* "I cannot help referring to Dr. Brooks's superb personal unconsciousness, which was a rare and striking quality in so popular a man. I once witnessed a striking example of this quality. It was at an exhibition at the Kindergarten for the Blind — that blessed institution which Dr. Brooks had so special an affection for. Many people, men and women, filled the rooms. Dr. Brooks had taken up poor

Interior of Trinity Church, Boston.

little deaf, dumb, and blind Tommy Stringer, who had just come to the Kindergarten, and who knew nothing whatever, but who seemed somehow to be aware when he had come close to a kind heart. He clung tightly about the big man's neck, like a little old-man-of-the-sea, and the remarkable thing about it was that Dr. Brooks did not seem in the least anxious to dislodge him, or at all disconcerted by his persistent attention. He went about with the poor boy clinging there ; he conversed with people without any sort of embarrassment, and also without that superior sort of condescension which almost any other great man would have exhibited under such circumstances. Afterward, speaking in Helen Kellar's behalf, he made an earnest appeal for Tommy."

The same writer said again : " No one has yet fully explained the secret of Dr. Brooks's hold upon the great mass of people who were not Episcopalians, who never saw him in private life, and who, perhaps, had never heard him speak but once or twice. Thousands of such people felt a sharp pull upon their heart-strings when they heard of his death. Probably a little of a good many things went to make up this sentiment. There was the feeling that the bishop was not only a wonderfully good man, but also a man of hearty human sympathies, and without cant or pretence. But that was more or less an abstract sentiment. My idea is that a great part of Dr. Brooks's popularity came from the mere sight of the man on the street or in other public places; and this is not in the slightest degree a depreciation of his greatness, for he would not have looked the man he did unless he had been the man he was. On the street he always had a certain splendid boyish unconsciousness — a natural and unaffected air of liking for the world and the people in it — which, joined with the magnificence of his stature, impressive to all except little men, made people's hearts warm toward him definitely and for all time. And when these same people saw him once or twice at a public meeting of some kind, and had seen his perfectly fitting bearing, and had listened to his perfectly fitting words so swiftly spoken, their liking was re-enforced by a strong admiration. Every one, Anglican or not, came to feel a sense of ownership in him. The influence which he wielded by reason of his peculiar and gifted personality made his episcopal office a little thing in comparison."

Bishop Brooks was only fifteen years old when he entered Harvard College, and at that time he was almost as tall as at any period in later life, although he had not developed into the magnificent specimen of physical manhood which he presented in later years.

Speaking of him, Mr. Robert Treat Paine said : " At college he cared little for sport, but preferred to read omnivorously almost everything and anything that came in his way. His literary work was marked, even then, by the same incisive, thorough-going style that we have become familiar with in his published sermons, and was nothing less than a natural gift which he cultivated at college to the highest point that wide reading would assist."

Mr. J. S. Ropes remembers distinctly the college boy's appearance at the initiation of the class of '57's representatives into "Alpha Delt." The bishop-to-be was lounging on a cushioned window-seat smoking his college pipe and watching the novitiates quizzically and quietly, till somebody had to break the ice. Then the big college student came down from his perch and charmed everybody with his frank, open personality. His manners were never made over to fit any new position he might attain, but were always the same from his college days.

One of the stories told relates to

some of the Lenten services held by Phillips Brooks when he was rector of Trinity Church. His friend, ex-Governor Rice, met him one morning in the street-car, and said, "Aren't you getting a little weary with the Lenten services?"

Dr. Brooks's face brightened as he replied, "I guess I can stand it if the congregation can."

When in England, he was "commanded" to preach before the Queen, and was asked on that occasion if he felt afraid to do so. He replied: "No; I have preached before my mother." When he visited England after his election as bishop he was warmly greeted and honored. It was "My Lord Bishop" here and "My Lord Bishop" there, and all the sturdy Americanism of Phillips Brooks rose in protest. "I am not a lord bishop!" he exclaimed; "we have no such titles in our country, and you will oblige me by not using that form of address."

The following is from Miss Lilian Whiting: —

"When he entered upon the pastorate of Trinity Church he found his field to lie in one of the most conservative and intensely aristocratic parishes of America. The pew-holding is from a a peculiar system of title-deeds almost,

and the prevailing spirit was rather to
resent than to invite the presence of
strangers. A story is still told that on
one Sunday a dame of high degree
coming late to service found her pew
occupied by two or three persons, although there was still room for her
accommodation. But, to the dismay
of the strangers, she waved them out,
one by one, with a grand sweep of the
ostrich feather fan which she carried,
and left them to their fate standing in
the aisle. The young preacher, from
his desk, saw this performance and pon-
dered upon its significance. My in-
formant, who was also an eye-witness
of the scene, tells me that a more in-
dignant man than the rector at that
moment could hardly be imagined.
From that time he resolved that, although by the parish laws the church
must still be one of rented pews, rather
than free, it must still rise to the true
spirit of Christian courtesy and hospitality. Nor were his efforts in vain,
and for many years Trinity has been
noted for its marked courtesy and generous hospitality — a hospitality, indeed, that so overflowed all considera-
tions of the right of possession that it
came to be laughingly remarked that
the unfortunate pew-owners seemed to
be the only persons who could not

be accommodated in Trinity. By the rector's desire a row of chairs was placed all around the chancel, and several long seats placed in rows on either side, all free to the occupants ; 'and as many as can come and sit in my pulpit with me are welcome,' characteristically asserted the rector."

During the last years of his life the members of the Harvard class of 1855, resident in Boston and its vicinity, were in the habit of dining together every two or three months. At these reunions youth seemed renewed, and all were like boys again. Phillips Brooks was almost always present at them, allowing nothing but the most unavoidable engagement to keep him away. In that room he always appeared to be the same charming, frank, simple-hearted boy he had been in undergraduate days, and never seemed to feel himself, or so far as he was concerned allow any one else to feel, that his rank, there or outside in the estimation of the world, was any different from that of the most insignificant or "unsuccessful" person present.

In conversation *à propos* of a clergyman who had been detected in some offence and had brought himself into disrepute, he once solemnly said : "How wretched I should be if I felt that I was carrying about with me any secret which

I would not be willing that all the world should know!" And indeed morally and socially he seemed perfectly transparent — as if one could look him through and through, and find nothing amiss.

He loved and admired Richardson, the architect. Looking at his design for the Pittsburg Jail, he said in his presence: "What Richardson really likes is a jail. When he can't get a jail, he wreaks himself on a church."

Towards the end of his life — it was thought by one whose opportunities of judging were excellent — he seemed, after having apparently long resisted the thought, to have at last yielded to the irresistible conviction that his position in, and the manner in which he was regarded by, the world were unusual. Only then did he consent to enter the episcopate. Yet this conviction was for him simply a stimulus to larger labor for others: it never led him to "give himself airs" towards them. As bishop he was as simple and genuine and unaffectedly devoted to well-doing as ever he had been as a boy.

Said a writer in the *Boston Globe:* "I stood on the curbstone on Clarendon Street the morning of the funeral, watching the great long line of humanity which was wending its way to the west porch of Trinity Church. By my side was an Irishman of perhaps sixty years of age. Addressing me he said, 'Well, he's gone, and Boston never saw a better man. He was a good man, generous, open, and liberal. I can well remember him as a young man taking his meals at the Parker House. This was twenty-seven years ago, and at that time I was a waiter at Parker's. Many a time I've served him. Did he remember the waiter? He never forgot him, and his remembrances were not those of a small soul, either. He was a lucky fellow who waited on Phillips Brooks.'"

Bishop Potter once said of him : —

"I first met Bishop Brooks while I was a student at the Alexandria Seminary. I had been there a year or two when he entered, and I recall a humorous incident of the time. He was quite a tall man. When he arrived there as a student he was placed in one of the rooms of the old building, the ceiling of which was so low that he could not stand erect. I heard of the awkwardness of his situation, and exerted such influence as I possessed to secure his removal to a hall some distance off, which was known as St. John's in the Wilderness, and so he came to be established there. He made a very apt and striking reference to this incident a few years ago on the occasion of my consecration as bishop. He said he hoped that it would continue to be Henry Potter's business to see that men stood up straight in the world.

" I recall an incident illustrating his simplicity. A member of the seminary, George A. Strong, was recorder at a parish at Medford, Mass., and upon one occasion Dr. Brooks and I were driving out there to see him. When we were crossing a railroad track one of the whiffletrees broke. I immediately jumped out of the carriage to repair the damage. But Brooks never stirred. There he sat looking at me with apparently no more concern than a wooden idol might be expected to have until, with some degree of impatience, I ordered him to get out and hold the horses' heads while I was making repairs. It had never occurred to him that he could be of the slightest use.

" I remarked to a gentleman afterward, ' It is astonishing how little Brooks knows about horses.' — ' Well,' said the gentleman in reply, ' he spoke much more handsomely of you, for he told me he was amazed to see how much Henry Potter knew about horses.'

" I watched him with great interest on the occasion of the recent convention of the House of Bishops in Baltimore. I knew how attention to details and the slow progress of legislation would weary him. His seat was far back among the younger bishops, as the bishops are always seated in the order of precedence with respect to the time of their election and consecration. I was not surprised, therefore, when passing along the aisle near where he sat I felt some one pulling at my skirts. I looked around and saw it was Brooks. Glancing up at me in that peculiar pleasant way of his, he asked, ' Henry, is it always as dull as this?' I leaned over and said to him, 'If you will be patient, my dear boy, you will find it animated enough.'

"I was not surprised, in the largest sense of the word, to hear of his death. He had for so many years lived a life of regularity as rector, to change from that routine suddenly, to take up and discharge the duties of a large diocese, involved a tremendous physical risk. He went into his work with his whole heart."

How fast the bishop talked is shown by the following interesting statement of the swiftest of English shorthand writers, Thomas Allen Reed, about his attempts to report the sermons preached by Rev. Phillips Brooks: " I have never, in a long and varied experience, listened

to a public orator, whether in the pulpit,
on the platform, or even in a law court,
where perhaps the fastest speaking is
heard, who kept up such a continuous,
uninterrupted flow of rapid articulation.
However large the building, the speed
of delivery is the same. Even the opening sentences, which many habitually
rapid speakers will utter quite deliber-
ately, are jerked out with the most pro-
voking glibness, and the reporter no
sooner puts pen to paper than he finds
himself dashing forward, helter skelter,
his energies taxed to the utmost to get
up and maintain the necessary speed.
He is eagerly expecting the end of the
first sentence, where he naturally antici-
pates a pause. Vain expectation! The
full stop is a grammatical expression ; it
has no reality for the speaker or the
writer. One sentence ended, the next
begins, and, like the Dutchman's cork
leg, the sermon 'goes on the same as
before.'

"Having recently had occasion to
report Mr. Brooks, I have had the curiosity to note his exact speed. The sermons were accurately timed (by two
watches in each case), and the words,
as they appeared in the printed report
in the *Christian World Pulpit*, were
counted. One sermon, preached at
Caterham, lasted thirty-five minutes,

and the average rate of speed came out at a hundred and ninety-four words per minute. But in a sermon preached in Westminster Abbey, Mr. Brooks exceeded even the rate of the Caterham sermon. Notwithstanding the size of the abbey, and the effort needed to articulate with sufficient distinctness to be heard, the sermon, which lasted thirty minutes, came out two hundred and thirteen words per minute. I repeat, then, if any aspiring young shorthand writer wishes to meet a foeman worthy of his steel (or any other) pen or pencil, let him take an opportunity of attacking the Rev. Phillips Brooks of Boston, and the chances are that at the close of the encounter he will find the taking of a Turkish bath a superfluous operation. Fortunately for the shorthand fraternity on this side of the Atlantic, Mr. Brooks does not often visit these shores. If he did, I am afraid that, instead of being cordially welcomed, he would be received, at least by the knights of the pen, with the greeting of the Quaker in ‘ Uncle Tom’s Cabin,’ ‘ Friend, thee isn’t wanted here.’ ”

His rapid delivery was one of the chief characteristics of the man, and to take him *verbatim* usually in this country required the work of two stenographers working in concert, the one filling in the gaps left by the other. It was in this way that the *verbatim* reports of his famous Lenten noon-day lectures at St. Paul's Church were made. His rapidity of speech was indulged in for the purpose of overcoming a lingual defect, and when he reached his topmost speed his effort was comparable to nothing except that of a steam-engine. Indeed, the phrase "a human dynamo," applied to another well-known clergyman, would also fit Bishop Brooks's case as well. Despite the rapid gait at which he talked, however, there was nothing involved or hazy about his spoken sermon, and it was easy to follow his line of thought when one had once got used to his mannerisms.

The memory of the stalwart figure standing in the pulpit, the rhythmic words flowing from his lips like a silvery cascade from a mountain, the face flushed, the eyes flashing, and the eye-glasses dropping downward with the unconscious twitching of the nose, will always be a pleasant and abiding one with the scores of newspaper men whose duty called them to report his utterances.

One of the swiftest of Boston's shorthand writers, and who has reported the bishop many times, said : —

" Bishop Brooks was the fastest talker

I ever reported. So many ideas on the subject under treatment would float to the surface of his mind in a second's time that the tongue seemed, as it were, too slow a vehicle to convey them to his audience, and with scarcely a comma's pause, the words would flow naturally forth, in a manner that suggested to the imaginative reporter undercurrents of more crowded ideas, which must follow in rapid succession. Another difficulty in reporting Bishop Brooks was the confidential tone he would assume, lowering his voice to almost a whisper, and leaving the reporter to transcribe his meaning out of a sort of impressive, though one might say eloquent, rumbling sound, and quickly changing facial expressions, but which, to one in the habit of hearing him, were sometimes as translatable as words."

One of the members of the Trinity Club, an organization composed largely of young men, tells the following, which he heard from Mr. Brooks's own lips as he narrated it in a moment of confidence. Speaking of his well-known rapidity of speech, he said that many people supposed that it was due to a habit of stammering when he was young, and that he avoided the defect by rapid utterance. Mr. Brooks said that the idea that he ever stammered or had any trouble

A CORNER OF TRINITY, BOSTON.

with his speech was entirely erroneous.
When he was young, he said, and began
public speaking, he was afraid that people would not hear him if he spoke at
much length, so he used to get as much
as possible into a short time, and this
intentional fast speaking became by
practice a permanent habit. Speaking
of the diffidence he felt on entering the
pulpit, he told his young friends that it
was something he could not shake off;
when he thought what a great responsi-
bility it was to preach to such a congregation, it gave him a feeling of dread
and hesitation in the extreme. " It is
something fearful " was the expression
which he used.

To the newspaper men of Boston
Bishop Brooks naturally bore a very important relation, and, in fact, he had
done so for a great many years. He
was easily the foremost preacher in this
part of the country, and his sermons and
addresses and social functions always
had a conspicuous place in the printed
news of the day.

No one had more respect for him
than the newspaper reporters, and yet
he was one of the most unapproachable
men from the standpoint of the inter-
viewer. He would always treat a newspaper man in a pleasantly dignified way,
but would seldom say anything for pub-

lication, his nature seeming to rebel against this particular form of publicity.

Before Dr. Brooks became bishop, his photographs, though much in demand, could not be had by every one. He was much averse to having them placed on public sale, and once, when he was asked to allow some to be sold at a fair in aid of St. Andrew's mission, he showed some disinclination to comply, and remarked that they would not realize much. This was met with the statement that it was expected that about fifty dollars would be the result of such a sale. The next day Dr. Brooks sent his check for fifty dollars to the managers of the fair, but the photographs were not forthcoming. At length he was prevailed upon to sit for his picture, and just before Christmas in 1887 he sat to a photographer in the Studio Building. Three positions were taken, and all were perfectly satisfactory, but the picture which proved the most attractive to the public, and the one which his parishioners greatly admired and were eager to possess, is the one showing the full face. During the eight months subsequent to the development and finishing of the negatives, more than three thousand photographs were sold. Two orders were for five hundred each. There has been a large sale ever since of all three positions, but the one especially sought after is the front position. In June, 1891, a private business arrangement was entered into with the photographer whereby a royalty was to be paid on each picture of the bishop sold, the proceeds to be used for mission purposes. This arrangement has been carried out according to the wishes of the bishop and his associates.

Whether a similar arrangement was entered into with the London photographers, who secured two fine negatives of the bishop while in England last year, is not known. Probably not. One of the pictures taken by the London artists represents Dr. Brooks sitting in a chair, with an open book on his knee ; the other shows him standing. Both are considered good likenesses. Conspicuous on each photograph are the lines, " The Lord Bishop of Massachusetts, the Rt. Rev. Phillips Brooks, D.D."

In the August, 1891, number of *Sun and Shade* is a beautiful reproduction of a photograph of the bishop standing in his library, a copy of the picture taken by Dr. Mixter.

A photograph from a painting of Dr. Brooks by Wallace Bryant, made in 1891, is published.

There are undoubtedly other photographs of the bishop, copies from originals, etc., other than the above and those reproduced in this volume.

One of the earliest incidents of Dr. Brooks's pastorate at Holy Trinity, Philadelphia, was the flurry of alarm in 1862 over the menace to that city from the near approach of the Confederate army. When the "three-months' men" were called out and the available forces remaining in the city were gathered together to protect the Quaker town, it was the stalwart figure of the young rector of Holy Trinity which was seen in the van of those marching out, shovel on his shoulder, to throw up protecting earthworks in front of Philadelphia.

Bishop Brooks, before he was consecrated to the episcopate, was generally known as a representative in Massachusetts of the "broad-church" party as opposed to the "high-church" tendencies. One day Dr. Brooks was walking in a long procession of clergymen who were attending some church festival of considerable importance. Beside Dr. Brooks in the procession walked a short, thin priest, Dr. Spalding. Dr. Spalding was at that time an extreme high churchman. As the procession moved along and approached the robing-room, Dr. Spalding looked up at Dr. Brooks, who towered above him, and said : "You are, after all, Dr. Brooks,

in some respects at least a *high* churchman." — "Yes," replied the rector of
Trinity, glancing at his own enormous
physique and then looking at the thin-
chested man beside him, "but in no
sense can you be called a *broad* churchman."

Just after the close of the war, it will
be remembered that there was a commemoration meeting at Harvard College. Phillips Brooks was asked to deliver the prayer. Colonel Henry Lee,
the Harvard marshal for that day, said,
"The services on that occasion were
not equal to what men felt. Every
thing fell short, and words seemed to
be too weak. Phillips Brooks's prayer
was an exception. That was a free
speaking to God, and it was the only
utterance of that day which filled out
its meaning to the full extent. Lowell's 'Commemoration Ode' was great,
and so was General Devens's speech, but
Mr. Brooks surpassed them both." The
eager inquiry of that day after that
prayer was "Who is Phillips Brooks?"
It was the first time that he had appeared before the most distinguished
audience that could be collected in New
England ; and from that moment the
growing thought at Trinity Church was
to call Phillips Brooks to be rector of
that church.

The following characterization is from a brilliant article in the *New York Tribune*, in 1884: "He is a Brahmin of the Brahmins so far as the intellectual caste of the man is concerned; and yet his individuality is crowded with perplexing contrarieties, for there is not a trace of his New England lineage to be found in an analysis of his springs of action or the outgrowth of his professional life. For while the New England cultus is cool, dry, crystalline, and rhythmic, his is hot, heady, effervescent, daring, spontaneous. Boston is Scandinavian, dashed with Teutonic. Mr. Brooks is half Mediterranean, half Oriental. He is severely scholastic in his discipline, but a tropical exuberance of glowing effervescences, with the hidden fire of compressed metaphors, pre-occupies and kindles his utterances. The New England ideal never loses sight of self, is always 'at home' with a stately deference for the conventionalities of schools and society, while · Mr. Brooks is verily possessed with an imperious and tremendous dæmon, as Plato interprets, and so is accountable to no man or precedent."

Said the *Boston Transcript*, in one of its editorials: "The famous John Cotton, minister in Boston in old England and New England, — in whose honor our city was named, — was a worthy ancestor

of Phillips Brooks; the famous Phillips
Academy was founded by another ancestor; the bequest from which have
been made the statues of Winthrop and
Samuel Adams was given to the city by
another ancestor.   But the greatest gift
to the city from any of his family was
Phillips Brooks — his own life and example, to which the good citizen, independent of city, State or national boun-
daries, rising above all differences of
religious creeds, pays universal homage
to-day.   Such homage proves that materialism has not swallowed up this
people."

VIII.

INFLUENCE WITH BUSINESS MEN.

AMONG the many thousands of people who will regard the death of Bishop Brooks as a personal loss are the business men of Boston whose privilege it was to attend the noon-day services in St. Paul's Church during the penitential seasons of 1891 and 1892, when he delivered two series of sermons remarkable alike for their fervent piety and for their adaptability to the every-day life of the busy men to whom they were addressed. All shades of belief were represented at these meetings, and many of the most interested listeners to the solemn truths he uttered probably had no settled religious convictions. But so broad was the mantle of Christian charity which he offered them, that it is doubtful if even the most intolerant sceptic did not find them suited to his needs. If any cavillers yet remained, the bold challenge was sent forth in the most meek and modest manner that the speaker himself would gladly listen to any objections that could be made to the doctrines which he taught, let them come from what source they might. He even went further than this in his famous declaration that he had as much respect for the opinions of the honest unbeliever, and could regard him with as much toleration, as though he was a professor of his own faith. Little wonder was it, then, that men who seldom or never attended church flocked at the busiest hour of a busy day to listen to one who welcomed them as sons of the same Father and brothers of the same Redeemer. To many it was a revelation that the greatest bishop of a great church could so near approach his Master in meekness and humbleness of spirit.

But these men were probably not more astonished and delighted than were those whose walks in life had been among the familiar paths of church dogma and creed. They learned — many of them for the first time — that the great representative of a church, which they had been taught to believe was made up of forms and ceremonials and rituals, cold and conventional, regarded all these

symbols of little consequence as compared with the vital truths of Christianity. With an eloquence and fervor that
carried conviction to every mind, he
swept aside as of little consequence
everything that had not for its essential
the all-pervading love of the Saviour of
the world for all mankind under whatever circumstances or in whatever condition of life it might be found. All
that was essential in Christianity was
that there should be some one to receive it. The Church was, to him, an
organization through the medium of
which revealed religion could be taught
and disseminated ; a religion that could
be found in all its integrity as readily in
the humble little chapels of the primitive Methodist as in the great temples
of Episcopalianism ; in the rude bar-
racks of the Salvation Army as in the
sumptuous cathedrals of the Holy City.
No wonder, then, that clergymen and
laity, churchmen and non-communicants,
believers and unbelievers, united in these
services, and approved of the great and
unanswerable truths announced.

He even went a step further in his
broad and comprehensive liberalism and
in his belief in the infinity and pres-
cience of God. It was not necessary,
he said, in the divine plan of salvation
that the sinner should consciously seek

God. And to emphasize this belief of his, he used the startling and striking metaphor of the prisoner in a dungeon cell so completely shut out from the light that he knew not of its existence. It was then that Bishop Brooks, in a great burst of eloquence, described as only he could describe the desperate seeking for the light that was so necessary for his very existence by the poor benighted wretch. He knew not whether it was night or day ; but there was that craving within him for the unseen light that with desperate energy he tore at the rough walls of his cell till the blood flowed from his lacerated fingers, and he sank exhausted, disheartened at the hopelessness of his ever reaching what his inner consciousness told him must exist, for it was essential for his growth and happiness. All this time, on the outside of these walls, the bright rays of the sun were seeking for the man who needed them so much. Every crevice between those great stones was filled with light and sunshine, which insinuated its life-giving properties into the most remote place in that gloomy mass of rock. The light which the prisoner sought so blindly, unconscious that it even existed, was as persistently seeking him. Such, said the preacher, is the relative position of

PHILLIPS BROOKS —
A ONCE FAMILIAR FIGURE ON BOSTON STREETS.

the sinner and his God. Knowing nothing of the existence of the Divine Mercy so essential to his salvation, the poor outcast is not deserted, for his God, like the sunlight of heaven, is constantly and persistently seeking him.

At such moments as these it seemed as though the great preacher was inspired, and men looked at him and wondered. Everything that he said evidently carried conviction to their souls. He pleaded with them only as a man thoroughly in earnest could plead, to lay aside their vices and tricky business methods, and become Christians. He pointed out to them the satisfaction and peace of mind that would come from leading a grander and better life. He told them it was no hardship to be a Christian; it was a pleasure and a delight, and his beaming, smiling countenance, as he made these appeals, told how completely happy he himself was. Christ, as he described him in these discourses, was not a mean and humble appearing personage, but so grand and lofty and magnificent that should he walk through the busy marts of trade all men would recognize in him the Saviour of the world.

During the two series of sermons St. Paul's Church was crowded long before the hour for the services to begin, and the rapt attention that accompanied every word that was spoken was the strongest commentary that could be made on the earnestness of the speaker and the conviction that his words carried to the hearts of men.

PHILLIPS BROOKS AT HARVARD.

IX.

PHILLIPS BROOKS AT HARVARD.

THE following appeared in *The Boston Transcript:* —

To most men it would be a sufficient task to fulfil the exacting requirements of such a pastorate as that of Trinity. Add to these requirements a wide range of philanthropic sympathies and endeavors, and also a very considerable amount of literary work, and the most energetic of men might consider that his powers were fully exercised. Phillips Brooks, in addition to accomplishing all this work, and accomplishing it most effectively, found time to make his influence felt at Harvard as no other preacher ever did.

It is of this latter work that the writer wishes to speak. During his junior and senior years he became very familiar with the sight of Phillips Brooks,

187

both in the chapel pulpit and upon the
college campus.   Many a morning, after
chapel, one might see President Eliot
and the great divine crossing the quad-
rangle together, or coming down the
avenue in front of Gore Hall.   President Eliot is himself a tall and stalwart
figure; but he was completely dwarfed
by the great bulk and towering height
of his companion.   Clad in a volumin-
ous ulster, with a large broad-brimmed
silk hat tipped back a little on his head,
and usually with a big walking-stick
under his arm, Dr. Brooks strode along
in Brobdingnagian ease, looking like a
walking tower.   His face in repose suggested benevolence and placidity rather
than power, and irreverent college
younglings used to comment wittily
on his habit of keeping his mouth ajar
as he walked along.   He was usually
wrapped in profound abstraction, often,
it is said, passing his best friends without recognition.

The system of "preachers to the university," which was established at the
time referred to, was an attempt to
supply what was felt to be a most serious lack in Harvard life.   Dr. Brooks
was one of those who had implicit
faith that plenty of spiritual life lay
dormant in the college; and he of all
men did the most to call that spiritual

life into conscious power and activity. The old notion that the students were like the inmates of Dotheboys Hall, and that the *alma mater* was a sort of Mrs. Squeers whose pleasant duty it was to call them up and dose them with the brimstone and treacle of compulsory religion, gave way at length to more enlightened ideas. Faith in the better nature of man, and in that craving for the bread of life which the husks of dogma will not satisfy, was the basis of the new movement. Compulsory prayers were abolished. A number of eminent preachers took turns in leading morning devotions, and the present system of university preaching was adopted.

The system is merely this, that some well-known preacher is invited to conduct morning prayers every day for a month, and during that month he also preaches each Sunday evening in Appleton Chapel; and on every week-day during the month, from nine o'clock in the morning until noon, he may be found in a study set apart for that purpose, where any student who may desire to consult him on any subject will be sure of a cordial welcome and friendly counsel. During his month the preacher is said to be " in residence." Invitation is extended, in the college bulletin, to all who choose to seek the acquaintanceship or assistance of the preacher. Thus, as month follows month, and one eminent preacher follows another, an unusual and valuable opportunity is afforded for students to get personally acquainted with men of wisdom and spiritual power. The students avail themselves freely of this privilege, and there can be no doubt that much good has resulted from it.

The writer well remembers the day when he sought the comfortable, attractive parlor in old Wadsworth House and knocked at the door. A hearty "come in" responded, and in a moment he stood face to face with Phillips Brooks. A cordial grasp of the hand, a few simple, kindly words of greeting, and the visitor felt quite at home. During the half-hour of conversation that followed much was said which will always remain with the student as both a pleasant memory and a valuable acquisition.

Theological doctrines were the natural subject of our talk. Suggestions of doubt and difficulty in regard to current dogma were met by sympathetic insight, by patient logic, by eloquent illustrations.

"We all know," said Dr. Brooks, "that life is a tangle of mysteries,— that the simplest phenomena of nature baffle us completely when we attempt to explain them. Men differ, and always will differ, about a thousand minor matters relating to religion and the Bible."

"But difference is not tolerated in ecclesiastical circles," was demurred. "We are told that certain beliefs which we find revolting to our reason must be accepted, if we would be identified with Christianity and Christian people."

The great brown eyes kindled, and a glow of enthusiasm lighted up the earnest face.

"Christianity is reasonable, or it is nothing. It cannot conflict with reason; it is a supplement to it. The truths of salvation best appeal to the heart. Sweep away sophisms and intricacies and ask yourself, What is Jesus Christ to me and to my life?"

"But a belief in miracles is not a trivial matter, nor can the reason be ignored in examining it. We either believe them or do not believe them. Many of us find it impossible to accept them on any terms."

"Miracles!" he exclaimed. "How many stumble over them, yet how simple and natural they are, and how unimportant!"

He clasped his knee and rocked back and forward, speaking at full speed, and swaying his head as the torrent of words fell from him.

"Miracles are marvels. Anything that we don't understand is a marvel. My power to produce fire by scratching a match is a tremendous marvel to any savage. From his standpoint I am actually possessed of the most unquestionable power of performing miracles. Whence comes my power? From my superior nature, from my higher development, from my better understanding of the laws of the universe. Given my higher development, and you would *expect* to find me able to do things miraculous, or marvellous, to the savage on his lower plane. So, given Jesus Christ and his vastly higher development, his immeasurable superiority to the wisest and best of us, we should *expect* to find that he had a grasp on laws of which we know nothing, and to be able to perform things wonderful in our sight. A man is not saved by his belief in miracles — no man ever was — no man ever will be. Speaking for myself, the miracles of the Old Testament have very little significance to me; I have no belief in them, and consider them of very little importance. The miracles of Jesus seem to me very reasonable and probable, though I cannot say that I consider them of any **vital** importance.

That Christ rose from the dead, I most earnestly believe, and I believe that he became the first-fruits of those who will rise to immortality and the presence of the Father. That is the vital question, my friend. What is Christ to you and your life? That Christ should work miracles is to me the most natural thing in the world. But what are outer miracles compared with the wondrous miracle of transformation which he can and does work in poor, weak, sinful human hearts? Christ in us, and we in Christ, and the immortality of love and worship, these are the vital things. It is this co-relation of the human and the Christ-like which has made him the Redeemer of men. I have no patience with carping criticisms, while the essential, vital, redemptive truth is wholly overlooked. But there is nothing coercive in Christianity, no fettering of the best and highest thought of which we are capable, no overriding of our common-sense or manly freedom of thought and utterance. It chains us, not by force, but by attractiveness. It subdues us because we yearn to be subdued by its power. The Divine in us reaches upward, and the divine above reaches downward, and the two mingle, and that is a living faith in a living Christ."

To have omitted all the punctuation

points from the above quotation would better have represented the rapidity and breathlessness of its utterance. The exact words that he used are not quoted, but the thoughts are substantially recorded.

Much more was said, but to the same purpose. Nothing simpler or more unassuming could be imagined. Two students at ease in their own room could not have discussed any subject more freely. I think that Dr. Brooks was incapable "of talking down" to any human being. He was always the friend, the modest counsellor, the affectionate elder brother.

The influence of such a man at Harvard was tremendous and was much needed. That intellectual paralysis and moral dry-rot which some of its wretched victims complacently style "Harvard indifference" could not endure the presence and inspiration of a man like Phillips Brooks. One of his last efforts was an appeal to educate *young* men to do something. He lamented that so many delayed entering upon the fight of life until they had passed the first flush of youthful ardor. Do something, he adjured them, do something, *do* something! It was his last appeal to young men.

Many who visited him in the parlor of

PHILLIPS BROOKS AND CANON FARRAR.

the Wadsworth House carried away a lasting impression of reverence and admiration.   He was practical as well as spiritual.   One student came to him with a practical difficulty — a controversy in which he was engaged with some other students.

The facts were stated.   "What shall I do about it?" inquired the student.

"Weed your*self* out of the matter for a moment, and then see how the case stands.   After that, if you are still in doubt I shall be glad to give you any advice I can."

No further advice was needed.

Another student, to whom Dr. Brooks quoted Christ for guidance in an affair of every-day life, hinted that this was a *practical* matter.   The great preacher looked at him a moment, and an amused twinkle came into his eye.

"I have always regarded Christ as an eminently practical man," said he mildly.

The student retired with some food for thought.

Dr. Brooks was not lacking in humor. It is said, I know not on what authority, that in lecturing before a class of theological students one day he confessed that making pastoral calls was a difficult matter, requiring much tact, and often giving rise to perplexing situations. Fond mothers, he said, would sometimes thrust their babies upon his notice, and he felt that he must compliment the little one or grieve the fond parent. But one's stock of praises soon runs out, and there are dangerous possibilities of invidious discrimination in praises. It is not always easy to think up just the right thing on the spur of the moment, especially if the baby happens to be unprepossessing. He had adopted one simple formula. When the baby was produced, he looked at it and exclaimed, " Well, that *is* a baby ! " This was strictly true in every case, and he never knew it to fail of giving satisfaction.

It is fitting that Harvard men should bear the bier of the loyal son of Harvard who did so much to show his filial gratitude. His place will not be filled. Such men are not found often. His influence will be long in fading from the minds and hearts of Harvard men. The serene yet enthusiastic nature of the man will be an eternal legacy to the university.

X.

SECRET OF HIS SUCCESS.

UNLESS it bring with it a sense of keen personal pain to the individual mind, the death of no man, however great, is genuinely mourned. How fares it with each one in person? Is the world distinctly the poorer and more prosaic to you yourself for this death? Has it left you bereft of a great inspiration to joy, love, and hope? Apart from the distinct, sorrowing yes! to these questions — the yes! spoken out of tens of thousands of sincere hearts — all in vain will the newspapers drape their columns in black and call upon the entire community to mourn. The community as a community, like the corporation as a corporation, has no heart to mourn with. It can issue the command for splendid public obsequies, and bring out trains of hired mourners in crape, but it cannot cause one genuine tear to flow. Only the tears of each separate man or woman of a mighty host swell into the flood which attests as reality the grief of the actual community these sorrowers themselves aggregate into.

When the intelligence of the death of Bishop Brooks was suddenly flashed out on the bulletin-boards, it caused a quick, startling arrest on the busy streets. Men and women spoke with bated breath; their voices were choked with emotion. " We have lost him; we have lost him; we shall never see or hear him again on earth!" was the universal exclamation. Not one of a thousand of these men and women had ever spoken a word with the great preacher, or ever expected to. But none the less the sense of personal loss, the sense of something priceless gone out of their individual lives, was sadly there. Where, then, lay the secret of all this?

A great deal of vague and profitless talk is indulged in over what is termed the quality of "personal magnetism" in a man. Here is one of those accepted phrases that are made to take the place of adequate thought, and to explain without the need of explanation. Will not the currents of the magnetic battery cause the nerves to quiver and the muscles to contract, even in a dead body?

Well, in the same way one man is magnetic, while another is not! Why not rather say one man has fervid passion, and another not ; one man glow of humanity, and another not ; one man a torrent of thought, emotion, imagination, and divine vision, and another not. No sham fire ever warmed a man, no painted food ever nourished him. Mass and momentum of being alone never threw vast throngs into sympathetic vibration with itself.

"The tragedy of life," says Emerson, "lies in the poverty of human endowment." Yes, in the poverty of human endowment, in the sadly self-confessed reality that men and women in the average have such puny bodies, such scant affections, such feeble grasp of thought, such torpid imaginations, that nothing inspiring is begotten of them — here lies the tragedy of human life. And yet there goes along with this self-consciousness in countless minds an unspeakable yearning for a richer and diviner experience. Ah ! if they could love more ardently, think more vigorously, see more glorious visions of faith and cheer. For lack of those their daily round is so largely a dreamy treadmill to them. In sad depression they respond to Tennyson's words : —

> " 'Tis life, of which our nerves are scant,
>   'Tis life, not death, for which we pant,
>   More life, and fuller, this we want."

Then in some happy hour these nerve-scant men and women find themselves brought into contact with a battery of life like that which was coiled away in Bishop Brooks. The superb body, with such tides of ruddy blood circulating through every artery and vein, the great brain, teeming with such freighted wealth of ideas, the immense emotional power flowing out like a fiery lava flood, the splendid spiritual imagination glorifying with a celestial "light that never was on sea or land" the commonest details of life, the capacity for breathless adoration which makes the presence of God or Christ ecstatic passion to him — here is the living, breathing image of what every poor, halting, half-made shred of humanity yearns for in his own heart of hearts. And the grand, unconscious man, wholly lost in his divine message, believes in it for them all, however narrow now in intellect or cramped in spirit. Health and vigor! Whole oceans of it are in God, in store for all who seek it. Range of mind! Not the high seraph's mighty thought, who countless years his God has sought, can faintly image forth what lies before each soul made in the image of the eternal reason. Love! It will flood in, tide on tide, as revelation after revelation of the Divine Fatherhood breaks through eternity upon each passionate heart.

No wonder the auditors of such a man are swept away. He is doing for them what they cannot do for themselves — charging them with the fervor of his own love, opening out to them his own glorious vistas, lifting them up on the wings of his own soaring imagination. And, best of all, he is doing it by quickening into action their own latent religious powers, by bringing into consciousness their own hidden spiritual endowment. Apart from the contagion of this great glowing man of being, they may not be able to keep up of themselves this sense of exaltation. But how great a thing do they feel it, what a beatitude never to be forgotten, to have been even for once in a lifetime lifted into such a higher realm of consciousness, and so made alive to what there really is within their being, which, under more favoring conditions than here on earth, God may lift to higher reaches!

This, then, and this alone, explains the sense of personal loss, of genuine private grief with which thousands received the intelligence of the death of Bishop Brooks. It was the grateful, unselfish tribute of the consciously halt and maimed and blind to one created so much more fully and grandly than themselves in the image of God; to one who all unconscious of it himself, was yet living prophecy to them of what, in the endless resources of God, shall be the final inheritance of all struggling souls.

IN ENGLISH EYES.

XI.

IN ENGLISH EYES.[1]

IN writing these words about my friend Dr. Phillips Brooks, I shall not pander to the curiosity which hungers for personal details, but shall mention those large and sunny qualities of heart and mind which make Dr. Brooks one of the most enviable and one of the most widely loved of men.

He was born in Boston on December 13, 1835, and is therefore fifty-five years old. He went to Harvard University, where he graduated in 1855; and, after taking his degree, he studied at a divinity school in Virginia, and was ordained in 1859. From 1859 to 1869 he labored in Philadelphia, and partly as rector of the principal church in that

[1] This chapter, written by the Venerable FREDERICK W. FARRAR, D.D., Archdeacon of Westminster, appeared in an English journal for young men in 1891.

city. In 1869 he was called to Boston, and for twenty-two years he has been rector of Trinity Church, in the city of his birth. The church is by far the finest ecclesiastical building in America, and was designed by an American architect of genius, Mr. Richardson, whose premature death was universally lamented. The church holds upward of two thousand people; and, as Boston is considered to be the most intellectual city in America, it is probable that the congregation to which Dr. Brooks has preached for so many years is representative of the best culture of the great Western Hemisphere. The members of that congregation are devotedly attached to their eminent pastor. It is undoubtedly the case, as Professor Bryce observes in his great work on America, that the average American clergyman is better off than the average English clergyman. Any rector who, like Dr. Brooks, has won the attachment of his hearers, is sure to be the frequent recipient of such generous acts of kindness as are exceedingly rare in England. A few years ago, thinking that he looked a little tired, some members of his parish met together, and at once begged of him to leave them for a year, and to travel in Europe and India, without once thinking of them; they

offered to pay *all* his expenses for the
year, and also to pay and provide for
his substitute during his absence. The
generous and noble offer was, I believe,
at once declined, except so far as leave
of absence was concerned ; for Dr.
Brooks has always been in comfortable
circumstances, and is still a bachelor. I
told him that in England a clergyman
might be worn out with overwork, and
his face assume a deathly pallor, and
that yet, in thousands of parishes, it
would not occur to those for whom he
was spending and being spent, to come
forward with such spontaneous consid-
erateness. "Oh," he replied, laughing,
" it was only because they were tired
of me, and wanted a little change ! "

When I was in America I was twice
the guest of Dr. Phillips Brooks in his
beautiful and delightful home in Clarendon Street, Boston. That home is full
of objects of interest which he has collected in his travels, and is replete with
comforts ; but the infinite charm of its
hospitality depends on the unaffected
kindness, the rich culture, and the never-
flagging brightness of spirit which char-
acterize the host himself.

Surrounded by admirers, he is wholly
unspoiled by their adulations. His in-
vincible manliness rises superior to all
mere flattery, while he enjoys — as any

good man may well enjoy — all honest and sincere appreciation. Dearer to him than the applause of thousands is the undying attachment of a small circle of intimate friends ; and no one who has met him in the familiar intercourse of this happy circle is likely to forget the Sunday evenings which he has spent in the rectory of Holy Trinity, Boston.

But all America knows and loves and is proud of Phillips Brooks. I travelled with him to various large towns, and it was delightful to see the enthusiasm which his presence evoked in every audience ; for his face and figure are universally known throughout the United States. He is a man of magnificent physique, at least six feet four high, and of proportionate mould. Ordinary men look mere children beside him. Whenever I appeared with him on any platform, there was sure to be a call for him, and this was most of all the case when he visited any university ; for young men usually know a man when they see him, and Phillips Brooks is every inch a man. There is nothing artificial about him.

The most cultivated and the ablest preacher in America, he is wholly free from self-consciousness, the artificial mannerism and the petty pomposities which mark the commonplace ecclesias-

RECTORY OF TRINITY CHURCH—NOW THE EPISCOPAL RESIDENCE.

tic in every country. He always acts and speaks like a man among men, and the youths of America, to whatever religious denomination they may belong, recognize in him a man who feels a deep sympathy with them in all their temptations and difficulties, and who has set them an example of that stainless chivalry and large-hearted tolerance which marks the true gentleman and the true Christian.

If there be any living man whose mere presence seems to dispel all acrimony and cynicism, it is he. He enjoys life with all the heartiness of a boy, and in this respect he resembles Dr. Norman McLeod. He has travelled widely, carrying everywhere a quick power of observation and a receptive spirit. Before he dies he hopes to have seen at least something of most regions of this fair world. The heat of summer and early autumn in the American cities is so intense that the great majority of the worshippers in the Episcopal churches of wealthy districts — and the poor are mainly Roman Catholics — spend some months among the mountains or by the sea. Many churches are closed, or have fewer services for an inappreciable fragment of their usual congregations. This is the reason why American clergymen can travel far more than we can.

In any ordinary gathering of a hundred English clergymen not more than two would have visited America; in any ordinary gathering of a hundred American clergy —and I met such gatherings frequently — there would scarcely be one who had not visited England. Few, however, have had the delights of such extensive journeys as have fallen to the lot of Dr. Phillips Brooks.

Dr. Brooks, like Robert Browning, "believes in the soul and is very sure of God." He has the keenest interest in the rising generation, and envies them the share which they will have, as "the trustees of posterity," in a future which he not only views without alarm, but with the most glowing spirit of optimism. He thinks that the progress of the human race, in all things beautiful and noble, has all the certainty of a law. While he has rejoiced — as it has been given few to rejoice, in all the rich beauties of a useful and honored life, his one regret is that the brevity of life will prevent him from witnessing the beauty of those far horizons, which, as he believes, will unfold themselves before the happy eyes of those who are young now. The age through which we and he have lived has been a very wonderful age; but he thinks that its wonders are but preludes to those that lie just beyond the entrance door of the age which is to come.

Sympathy for all that is human, sunny geniality, unquenchable hopefulness, delight in all that is good and beautiful, a quick sense of humor, a large breadth of views, and the difficult combination of intense personal convictions with absolute respect and tolerance for the views of others, are the distinguishing features of his intellectual and spiritual character. They give to him the personal fascination which not even his opponents can resist. The High Church party in America look on his views with scant patience, and he has had to bear the brunt of their bitter criticisms; yet when one of the Cowley Fathers was elected to a bishopric, he found a supporter in Dr. Brooks, who knows that opinions must differ, and that there is room for diversity of methods and views in the divine charity of the Church of God. He is one of those men to whom the Americans apply the epithet " magnetic," and his very recent election to the bishopric of Massachusetts was received with a perfect storm of enthusiasm by men of all shades of thought.

In England he was first heard in Westminster Abbey and in St. Margaret's church. In St. Margaret's many of the first men in the kingdom came to hear him. He has since been invited to preach before the Queen and at both the Universities. Many of those who have listened to his large utterances must have felt that if we had even four or five such men as he in the Church of England, the atmosphere of her ecclesiastical assemblies would be more sunny and less suffocating than it sometimes tends to become. But I cannot recall the name of a single divine among us, of any rank, who either equals him as a preacher, or has the large sympathies and the rich endowments which distinguish him as a man.

As a preacher, he is marked by a certain fervid impetuosity, which reminds the hearer of an express train sweeping all minor obstacles out of its path in its headlong rush. His utterance is exceptionally rapid. He speaks many more words in a minute than our most rapid orators, and reduces reporters to absolute despair. This is so far a defect that it is exceedingly difficult for the hearer to keep pace with the sequence of his thoughts, conveyed, as they often are, in language of great beauty. The term " popular preacher" is mixed up with so many connotations of superficiality, of effeminacy, of vanity, of emptiness, of verbosity, that any

one to whom it is applied may well regard it as a term of humiliating insult.
But Dr. Brooks is most popular as a
preacher, and yet has gained his popularity by qualities the very opposite of
those which are supposed to attract congregations of young ladies and enrap-
tured devotees.   He is thoughtful, plain
spoken, fearless, essentially manful, and
entirely alien from the petty tricks and
intrigues which are too often visible in
the favorites and fuglemen of parties.
I have no space to enter into his style
or his theology ; but if my readers wish
to be brought face to face with teaching
which is profoundly and genuinely religious, with no trace of artificial scholas-
ticism, or the phrases and shibboleths
and half-truths of party theology ; if we
want to know something of Christianity
as Christ taught it, before it was corrupted by a thousand alien influences
of sacerdotalism and ecclesiasticism, let
them read the books of Dr. Phillips
Brooks on " Tolerance," and on the
" Influence of Jesus," or his three volumes of sermons preached in English
and American churches.   Such books
may serve to sweep away many cobwebs,
and to show them that, as the great divine, Benjamin Whichcot, said, " Religion means, above all, a good mind and
a good life."

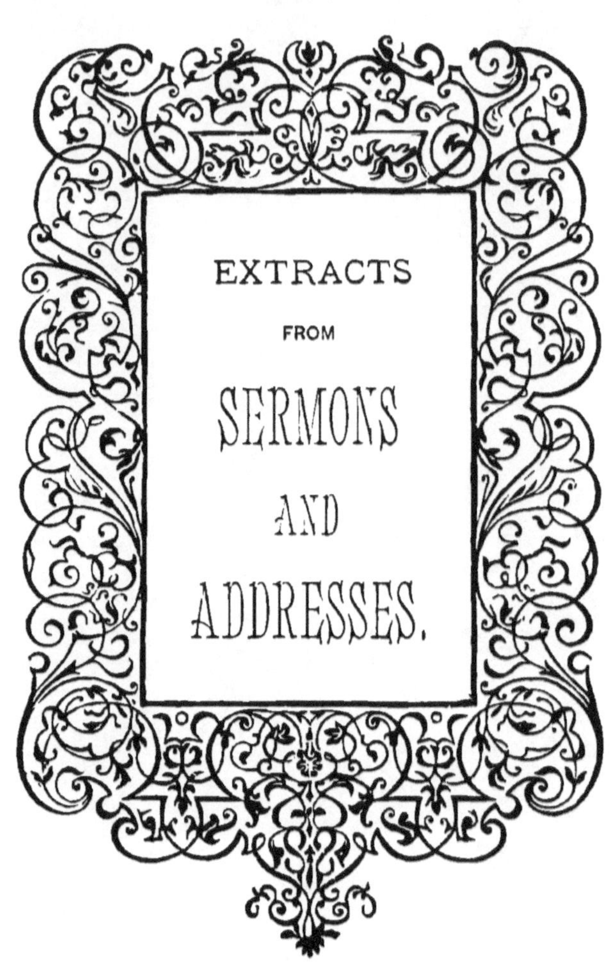

EXTRACTS
FROM
SERMONS
AND
ADDRESSES.

TO PHILLIPS BROOKS.

ON HIS ELECTION TO THE VACANT SEE OF MASSACHUSETTS.

Noluimus Episcopari te :
" Shepherd and bishop of our souls ! '' we said
When men gave *thy* name for the vacant see,
" Thou shalt not leave thy people ! '' — yet thou
       went'st.
So long had we abundantly been fed
On goodly pasturage, and snugly fenced
In our own fold, that selfishness was bred;
Like those in Jésh-urun we kicked against
The course that called thee to a broader field;
This was our error, for a power like thine
Should not be bounded by one flock and sealed
To special service; therefore we resign
Our claim, and like good Christians cheerly cry
" Give thee good bishopric ! — but not good-by.''

T. W. PARSONS.

MAY 1, 1891.

CONTENTS.

Education.

THE true future does not repeat but enlarges the present. And every present which accepts this law accepts with it its appointed work, to gather the stones and the timbers for the temples which the future is to build. It makes this the principle on which it proceeds in training a new generation. It disciplines the child with reverence, as destined to a completer life than the parent. It transcends selfishness, and prejudice, and jealousy, and, with a large and loving hope, a complete faith in human progress, it imagines no perfection for

itself except this relative one of perfectly
filling its place in the gradual perfection
of the whole.

You will see how this truth, which
makes the teacher in this great world-
school always recognize that the scholar
is to have larger work than his to do,
will make all education of necessity a
profound and thorough thing. It insists
on teaching principles and truths, and is
not satisfied with just imposing forms.

We look back over history, and we
see the same sight always. Wherever any
age has given its successor nothing but
forms and institutions ready-made, the
new age has not merely made no ad-

vance upon the old; it has invariably
shrunk and shriveled till it lived a life
too small even to fill the narrow limits
which its father claimed.   But wherever
any age has given its child an education
in any vital truths, the child has always
taken those truths, developed them into
an effectiveness and built them into a
beauty that the father never guessed.

THE Jew was so used to the sublime
thought of human life held fast in the
hands of the Divine authority, shaped
into gradual rectitude by the continual
pressure of command and prohibition;
the decalogue so supremely represented
to him the first thought of religion, that
his prayer for a new generation's religious life touched of necessity first of all

upon the moral side, the keeping of the commandments of the Lord. And here, I take it, the Jew simply conceives the course of all successful culture.

THE order of the Testaments is not an accidental, but an essential order. Calvary, in its idea, in its divine conception was "from the foundation," long before Sinai; but in man's apprehension of them, Sinai antedated Calvary by fifteen hundred years. The conscience must bow itself to the supreme " Thou shalt " and " Thou shalt not" of authority, before grace can enter in to win the heart with the gentle persuasiveness of its "Believe and live." John the Baptist must preach repentance before Christ can proclaim regeneration.

God wastes no history. In every age and every land He is working for the elucidation of some moral truth, some riper culture for the character of man.

The State.

GOVERNMENT is an incorporated, an embodied truth. Get any high idea about it, get beyond the thought that a nation is just a multitude of men who have happened to come together in a certain country, and who have bargained among themselves not to hurt each other, not to rob and kill each other, and you must come to this, that every nation is a divine utterance before the world of certain principles, of providence, of brotherhood, of justice, of the divine and human lives. The highest conception of the state, as of the world, is that it is an uttered thought of God, a certain colossal utterance of truth.

THE healthy state, like the healthy human body, can tolerate nothing within it that will not become part and parcel of itself, ready to share its fortunes, ready to do its work. A scholarship which tries to live in the state and yet not be of it, setting itself apart, fastidious, critical, captious, however thorough or elegant it may be, is mischievous. The politician who lives the life to which all politicians tend, of isolation from the common public interests, thinking that the state and government are things for him to use, and not that he is their instrument; that they exist for him, not he for them,—he is a terrible curse always. May God rid us of him speedily.

A GREAT public life moving healthily

will warn us of any coming dangers, as the ocean itself rings the storm-bell that tells of its own tumults.

THE time has . . . passed when a Sunday-school book need count it unworthy of its pages to help some boy in the city or on the prairies to gather up, with the love of the Lord who is to save him, a love of the land he may be called to die for, and of all the great race to which, if he lives at all worthily, his life is to be given.

I PLEAD with you for all that makes strong citizens. First, clear convictions, deep, careful, patient study of the government under which we live, until you not merely believe it is the best in all the world, but know why you believe. And then a clear conscience, as clear in private interests, as much ashamed of public as of private sin, as ready to hate and rebuke and vote down corruption in the state, in your own party, as you would be in your own store or church; as ready to bring the one as the other to the judgment of a living God. And then unselfishness: an earnest and exalted sense that you are for the land, and not alone the land for you; something of the self-sacrifice which they showed who died for us from '61 to '65. And then activity: the readiness to wake and watch and do a citizen's work untiringly, counting it as base not to vote at an election, not to work against a bad official, or to work for a good one, as it would have been to shirk a battle in the war. Such strong citizenship let there be among us; such knightly doing of our duties on the field of peace.

A STATE is not merely an idea, or an accident, or a machine, but is a being with the privilege of force.

SOMEWHERE, sometimes, it will assert itself strongly in the action of the world. Busied mostly within itself, in its own self-regulation, in the development of its own resources, and in the extension of its influence through the peaceful machineries of commerce and negotiation, there must be in it a power to enforce itself at the call of justice upon the unwilling action either of its own

subjects who separate themselves in rebellion from it, or against other nations
who wantonly set themselves in the way
of its just growth.

SINCE truth lives in outward struc-
tures, and embodies itself in govern-
ments, it has not merely its spiritual
relations to wills, but its physical relations to actions. It is hindered not only
by unconverted hearts, but by armed
rebellions. And so it has a right and
need to say not merely to the will
" Believe," but to the action " Submit."
It has not merely its higher functions of
persuasion, but its lower functions, too,
of *force*.

War.

H, how alike all history seems! How old, and yet eternally how new, these elementary emotions are! How the first instincts that make men fight for freedom, and good government, and truth, last on from age to age! old and yet ever young, like the eternal skies, the ever self-renewing trees, the gray and child-like sea!

DISPERSING armies and hanging traitors, imperatively as justice and necessity may demand them both, are not the killing of the spirit out of which they sprang.

IT is not the least of the debts that we owe to our Union soldiers that their very graves are vocal—that though dead they speak to us still.

THE men who from the bloody shore of the Rebellion embarked into the other life have left their foot-prints ineffaceable upon the margin where they planted them, and made it recognizable and dear forever.

IT is because in them, in what they were and what they did, the best of our national character shone out, that these soldiers have won a dearness and a permanent memory that do not belong merely to their personality. The nation honors in them its truest representatives. The real life of the land sees in them the ideal life which is the true outcome of its institutions. They were the flower of its principles, and so it sprinkles its memorial flowers on their graves.

IT was a noble gift of Providence that in one man [Washington] should be comprised and pictured, for the dullest eyes to see, the majesty and meaning of the struggle that gave our nation birth.

OH, the mysterious power of a death for a noble cause! The life is truly given. It passes out of the dying body into the cause, which lives anew.

WHEN the great ship had hardly
rounded into port; while, standing on
the shore of peace, we felt the solid earth
still rocking under our feet with the remembered heaving of the sea, they who
had watched and labored for her safety
through the nights and storms out on
mid-ocean, one by one, as if their work
was done, began to pass to their reward,
and to what other tasks we cannot know,
awaiting them in other worlds. What
have they left behind them, they and the
humbler dead whom votive monuments
and tender hearts remember still in every
town and hamlet of their land? Not
only what they did, not only even what
they were, but new tasks like their own
for us who stay behind them. They did
not merely clear the field of treason.
By the same labor they built up a new
possibility of national character and life.

They were like the men who, in these stony pastures of Andover, clear the rough field of stones and build the gray wall that is to surround and shelter it, out of the same material, at the same time. . . . . By purer social life, by finer aspirations, by more unselfishness, by heartier hatred of corruption, let us be worthy of them, and in our quiet duties build the true memorial to the characters of those who found their duty in the camp, the prison and the field, and where they found it did it even to the death. They saw that their country was like a precious vase of rarest porcelain, priceless while it was whole, valueless if it was broken into fragments. What they died to keep whole, may we in our several places live to keep holy! So may we be worthy of them.

As the merchant, the scholar, the
statesman, the diplomatist represent the
other elements of power in the state, by
which she impresses her will upon other
wills; so the soldier represents the element of force by which she must be
ready to rule action without ruling will
when the clear need shall come.

A MERCIFUL Providence kept our first
history from becoming a military history.
And if we ask how Providence did this
good work for us, the answer can be only
in the way in which God made the
thought and the devotion of the time so
strong that force was always kept in its
true place, — their servant.

His [the Puritan soldier's] was the great, homely, intelligible utterance of strength, ringing out clear and sharp in the midst of the often thin and over-subtle theologizings of the time, as the dazzling and bewildered atmosphere compresses and discharges its electricity in the piercing lightning and the pealing thunder.

When we look at Washington, we are at once struck by seeing how in him, who represented as a military man the force of the new ideas which were at work, we have also as a thinker, as a statesman and political philosopher, the clearest example of the reason of which that force was the expression. Often the two are disunited. One man does the thinking, another man does the fighting. One man develops the idea in the closet, and another makes it forcible upon the field. Rarely have the two so met in one man. Washington was at once the clearest thinker and the most effective soldier of our Revolutionary struggle.

NEVER was there a fighting-man with less of the purely military passion. He was the armed citizen, armed for a cause that belonged to the very essence of his citizenship. When that cause had triumphed on the field of battle, he laid down his arms and was the unarmed citizen,— the citizen, the same man still contending for precisely the same cause on the field of statesmanlike debate for which he had fought at Trenton and suffered at Valley Forge.

TRUTH in her armor is apt to be a very clumsy giant. Men will forget or deny what must be our belief all through, that the divine mission of force implies that force has no mission save for divine tasks, none for the mere brutalities of selfishness, or ambition, or jealousy, or worldly rage; none for the mere punctilios of national dignity.

FORCE has no right here in the world except as it is simply truth in armor.

THE presence of the distinct military element, the ruler of, or the slave of, but not a part of the nation, not bound up in the nation's fortune, nor sharing the nation's feeling, not springing from the nation's heart, this is what has made the weakness, and at last brought the death of many a noble nation, both of the old and of the modern times. May God save us from it forever.

IT is not necessary to excuse all our people's early or later treatment of the Indian. From earliest to latest — from the Pilgrim times down to the Indian policies of these last days—there is too much that never can be excused.

WE are suffering to-day [June 5, 1864], whatever be the secondary causes, for the violation of two of God's great moral laws, the law of the sacredness of govern- _nt and the law of the brotherhood of man. Gradually, grandly, from between these fearful wheels that drip with blood, are being ground forth into shapes which men's eyes, quick-sighted with anxiety, must see, these two eternal ordinances of God, that government has a divine right to be honored, and that man has a divine right to be free. Those two truths, burned into the very fibre of our people as they walk the fire, are to be the great moral acquisition of American character.

Is there one of us that can look about him and think without a shudder of another generation of our people working out this same education that we are going through? What! all these fearful years again? Again these battles that the eye cannot count or the heart remember?   Again this waste of precious blood, this bitter hatred, these wild blazings-up of the devilish in man, this land with State on State where the harvests find no room to grow for the crowded graves? Must it all come again, this dark Egyptian Passover-night of history, wherein God leads the bondmen out, and, in all the stricken land that held them slaves, leaves in their deliverance "not a house where there is not one dead"? We have no right to leave a chance behind us that this work will have to be done again. But it must be, unless we can bring out of it all, clearly and definitely and forever settled, and lay down before the next age of Americans, the truths of national authority and human liberty, to be the materials out of which it is to build the future.

A TRUTH starts on its way across the world, sent by God to possess the world ; and that truth meets its obstacles,— obstinate and resisting men. It lays itself against the wills of those men. By every method of approach, through the affections and the conscience and the sense of beauty, and in every other way, it tries to get power over those wills and make them yield to it. It tries to rule the will and so to reach the actions which will be spontaneously obedient when the will has once submitted. It largely succeeds. That is the success it most desires. But when its efforts of persuasion and conviction have failed to remove any one obstinate enemy out of its path, what then? Surely, unless physical force be of a wholly immoral nature, we must believe that God has so arranged his universe that this beleaguered and hindered truth may claim the powers that can compel the action even when they cannot turn the will, and force out of its way an enemy who will not turn into a friend.

The Church.

O ! it dawns upon you that the Church is not to be made, that the Church is here already. In the aggregate of all this Christly life you have the Church of Christ, just as truly as in the aggregate of human existence you have humanity. One has no more to be made than the other. Both exist in their components.

THE Romish idea is that the Church thinks and struggles and receives help and revelation. The Protestant idea is that thought and struggle and help and light come to the Man.

THE living souls must go before the living Church, which has no life except in them. . . . Churches live in their souls. O, the old struggles, so endless and so fruitless, that history has to show, of men and times that tried to keep a Church alive without caring for the life of souls; men and times which seem to have strangely fancied that there was a certain power of vitality in the very Church itself, so that every soul on earth might cease to receive inflow of Christ and yet somehow the Church live on! It is the danger of the ecclesiastical spirit. It is the danger for all Churchmen and all Church times to fear.

THE Church, whose purpose in being is merely to feed her children's life and so increase her own, may harm the very life that she was meant to cultivate. This is nothing strange. Nothing is so likely to stop a stream of water as the broken or displaced fragments of the very earthen pipe through which it was meant to flow.

IF a Church, in any way, by hindering the free play of human thoughtfulness upon religious things, by clothing with mysterious reverence, and so shutting out from the region of thought and study, acts and truths which can be thoroughly used only as they are growingly understood, by limiting within hard and minute and invariable doctrinal statements the variety of the relations of the human experience to God, if, in any such way,

a Church hinders at all the free inflow of
every new light which God is waiting to
give to the souls of men as fast as they
are ready to receive it, just so far she
blinds and wrongs her children's intelligence and weakens her own vitality.
This is the suicide of Dogmatism.

IF, again, a Church, in any way, sets
any technical command of hers to stand
so across the path, that a command of
God cannot get free access to the will of
any of the least of all God's people; if
there be, as there has been again and
again, a system of ecclesiastical morality
different from the eternal morality which
lies above the Church, between the soul
and God, a morality which hides some
eternal duties and winks at some eternal

sins, just so far as there is any such ob-
liquity turning aside the straight, bright
ray that is darting right from the throne
of the God-soul to the will of the Man-
soul, just so far the Church maims and
wrongs her children's consciences, and
weakens her own vitality. This is the
suicide of Corruption.

AGAIN, if the symbols of the Church,
which ought to convey God's love to
man, become so hard that the love does
not find its way through them, and they
stand as splendid screens between the
Soul and the Love, or have such a positive character of their own, so far forget
their simple duty of pure transparency
and mere transmis.'   that they send
the Love down to the ,oul colored with

themselves, formalized and artificial; if the Church dares either to limit into certain material channels, or to bind to certain forms of expression, that love of God which is as spiritual and as free as God, then yet again she is false to her duty, she binds and wrongs her children's loving hearts, and once again she weakens her own vitality.   This is the suicide of Formalism.

THE time must come when Religion shall no longer make artificial virtues and vices of her own, and when with more unsparing tongue she shall detect and praise or denounce those virtues and vices which are essential and eternally the same.   Then a thousand rills of life will be open into her which are closed to-day, and she will live a thousand-fold.

OF the essential life of the Church, of the truly living Church, what can we say but this, that it is that which most completely feels that it was made for men, not men for it; which, therefore, lives only as it lives in them; which strives for nothing but to open more and more the channels of life from Christ to them? In such a church and such a church alone can be real unity. To be full of such a care for, and spirit of servantship to, the human soul, is the only power that can keep our own Church one in the midst of all her distractions. No outer bond of history or government can permanently hold her. Only this common purpose, freely working in the Church at large, can keep the true organic unity of life, which is the only unity worth having. The live pomegranate holds itself together with no

string tied round it. The dead pomegranate cracks and breaks. No tight-
est string can hold it. The Living
Church of truth, obedience, and spiritual
love, will guard its own integrity. The
disintegration of error, corruption or
formalism, what compactest system can
withstand !

THE Church does not become the
world's savior by furnishing it with a
powerful police.

THE true relations between moral law
and religious life are certainly not so
difficult as men have made them. Moral
action is, in one sense, the end ; that is,
it is the necessary result of religion, not
its final purpose. In another sense,
moral law is the means by which the

religious impulse steadies and supports itself, and mounts to higher spiritual heights. In this last sense, it is the very highest order of machinery, but it is machinery still. So that even if the Church were, what she has tried to be often, and has sometimes been to some extent, the great Reformer, breaking down sins, turning wrongs into rights, ruling men's actions everywhere; glorious as such a sight would be, it would not be the Church communicating life. She would be purifying and cultivating her own life. She would be making the world ready for the life she had to give it, but not giving it yet.

WONDERFULLY adapted to be the channel of the highest devotion, the deepest utterance of faith, submission and repentance, the very perfect machinery of Christian living, the Church system is dead without some power of Christian life.

So again of every sacred rite which, through the senses, opens a way for power to reach the heart. It is machinery still. The sensuous impression may make the soul receptive, no doubt it does, to some of the more external messages of God. But the impression itself is not soul-life. It is not a new birth, though its frightened or ecstatic shiver is easily enough mistaken for another Genesis.

WHO of us has not seen, nay, who of us in the deader moments of his parish life has not done, Church work enough --Sunday-schools, Bible-classes, night-schools, parish visiting, mothers' meetings and reading-rooms and all that — which he knew was only the mechanical whirling of the spindles by hand, with the vital fires utterly gone out in the furnaces below.

WHAT shall we say of Preaching? Only that if men can preach, and preach the very truth of Christ, year after year, and yet souls, thirsty for the water of life, sit at the dry mouths of their well-built channels and thirst in vain for help and salvation, then it must be that the mere telling the Truth as the mind can understand it and the lips can speak it, is not necessarily the communication of the Gospel Life.

THE Church . . . needs more of the Lord; more knowledge, more obedience, more love of Jesus Christ. Unless we get that, and make that bear upon men's hearts and souls, we may chant our own sweetest praises in their ears, and our appeal for sympathy will be only very piteous. It will sound to the world as the plaintive cries of the Church do sound to many men under their windows, like the beggar's violin, which neither claims tribute by the right of a governor, nor wins acknowledgment by the skill of an artist, but only extorts charity by the forlornness of the mendicant.

IF behind muscles, and blood, and brain, you know that there is a vital force, which utters itself through them, but which is another thing than they, which would live even if they were dead, then it is not strange to say that behind all morality, and order, and rites, and work, and preaching, there is a vital power of the Church, which utters itself through them, but which is another thing than they, without which they were dead, but which might live though every one of them should die. That life-power is Christ always entering into the Church, as truth, and guidance, and love; and always passing out from the Church into humanity by the otherwise dead functions, vitalized by Him, of teaching and government, and active work.

As in the world of science men fear materialism which would crowd spirit and vital force out of the universe, and make all life exist and spread itself in the mechanical arrangement and re-arrangement of material atoms; so there is always fear, and never more fear than now, of an ecclesiastical materialism, which shall make little of spiritual force, and try by the mechanical arrangement and re-arrangement of ecclesiastical atoms, of dioceses, and conventions, and canons, and rubrics, and the like, to make the dead world live the life of God. Such a materialism turns machineries from being the homes into being the tombs of force, and makes us dread each step we see it take in advance.

IF ever our Church goes back, and cumbers herself with the precedents, and submits herself to the influence or author- ity, of the English Church, her power in this land is gone. She must be part and parcel of this people. She must be in heart and soul American, or she is noth- ing. She must have her sympathies here, and not across the sea. She must have her gaze and enthusiasm fixed upon the future of America, and not upon the past of England.

WE can conceive of a parish going on, the same parish still, though thought shall change and all religious speculation flow in new channels. But if men's souls cease to repent, and trust, and live by the divine communion, all is gone; the

Church is dead; the spiritual building crumbles in decay.

I KNOW that you will more than accept under the great, glowing, all-embracing hospitality of this bounteous roof [that of Trinity Church, Boston], you will enthusiastically assert, that such a Church as this has no right to exist, or to think that it exists, for any limited company who own its pews. It would not be a Christian parish if it harbored such a thought. No, let the world come in. Let all men hear, if they will, the truths we love. Let no soul go unsaved through any selfishness of ours.

THIS is the modern notion of a Church, — not luxury, but work.

ANY man or any institution which attempts a great religious work in behalf of the growing generations of a country, must undertake, as preparatory to it, and as a necessary part of it, a great moral work as well. A faithful ministry, we hold, must not merely declare the Savior, but must attack and beat down those special sins which stand in the very door-ways and keep the Savior out of the hearts of men.

THERE are cases in which the move-ment of the will is everything; where to move action without moving will is to fail entirely. In such cases there can be no room for force. This is why our Lord, founding a religion whose whole life was to be in converted wills, found

no place in its establishment or propaga-
tion for the sword.

THE Church has been spread by force,
but Christianity never.   To try to think
of extending a faith by force, is to try
to think a contradiction.   It is like
thinking of raising enthusiasm with levers,
or crushing genius with sledge-hammers.
The tools have no relation to the material or the task.

I LOOK round on the work to do, and
I do not believe that either Episcopalianism or Methodism or Presbyterianism
or Baptism is going to assert the victory
of Christianity over sin, the opening of
the barred citadel of wickedness in this our

land. The Church of Christ, simple, unimpeded, armed powerfully because
armed lightly, the essential Church of
Christ must make the first entrance.
Then let us have up our methods of denominational government, and each, in
the way that he thinks most divine, strive
for the perfected dominion of our one
great Lord.

JUST as in God's great sea there is a
tide-power and a wave-power, and both
are the outputtings of the one same
force; just as neither denies the other,
each lends the other impulse; and the
quick waves, which fall like lashes, and
the slow, heaving, laboring tide, have
both their work to do in the eternal battle of the sea upon the land: so it is not
inconceivable that in the Christian world

there may be a church-force and a de-
nomination-force, which yet are both the
expression of one same purpose and design of Deity.

THE waves that crest themselves with
angry foam, and beat and beat and beat
from sunrise round to sunrise endlessly
upon the stubborn beach, are the most
visible agents of the work that is done.
But who will find anything but thankful-
ness, if once in every world-day the great
hand of the Maker and the Watcher is ·
put down under the great mass of the
sea itself, and the deep tide of Christian
law and Christian truth, with all the
waves running their eager races on its
bosom, is driven, mightily, silently, far-
ther up than any wave had reached upon
the conquered shore? Who will com-

plain if Christian union, for certain purposes, in certain efforts, develops a new
sort of power that the narrower individuality of denominational life has not attained?

THE everlasting principle remains, that
no moral authority or doctrinal correct-
ness or spiritual impulse can last from
generation to generation unimpaired, unless it incorporates itself in some recognized manifestation, and yields to the
crystallization which its essential life demands.

Scepticism.

HE countless assaults of a speculative time, testing every approach, bringing the manifold artillery of modern knowledge to bear, calling both the frivolity and the earnestness of our strange age to its aid, enlisting an internal treason as well as an external enmity — no wonder that they make the boldest fear sometimes. The rain is descending, the floods are coming, the winds are blowing and beating, and when loose houses are sliding off the slippery sand on every side of them, no wonder that the dwellers in the house upon the rock, with dazzled eyes, think sometimes that they see their own foundation waver. And yet the case does not seem hard to understand.

CHRISTIANITY is one and everlasting. Its work of salvation for man's soul is the same blessed work forever. But its relation to the world's life at large must be forever changing with the changes of that world's needs and seekings. The larger applications of Christianity must of necessity be from time to time readjusted, and in their readjustments its power may be temporarily obscured or unrecognized as it passes into new forms of exhibition. Is it strange, then, in a day of readjustments such as ours, when so many forms are going to pieces, so many old relations broken up and changed for new ones, when so many of the accidents of Christianity are being taken down, that men should be ready enough to think that Christianity itself is worn out and obsolete?

WE feel no doubt of the eternal issue. Our faith in Christ comes not from seeing how men treat Him, but from reading what God says of Him and feeling how He works. We are sure of the end; that all this overturning, overturning, overturning, must bring at last the day of Him whose right it is.

MEANWHILE, what can we do but keep alive by earnest and continual

utterance those truths which we believe,
no matter how utterly men may disown
their names, are doing the work of the
world all the while?   This is one of the
great values of such a time, that it sifts
and ordinates truths, and makes us find
out which are the few precious ones
that we will not let go at any risk.

And when we look about and ask,
How can we best preserve these truths?
I think there can be but one answer.
The highest truth has always found its
own best guardians.   Christ Himself
pointed to the younger generation that
was growing up about Him, and declared
its hands to be the place where His gospel would be safest, purest and most
fruitful.   Other years have their work to

do — old age, and middle manhood, and the fresh enterprise of originating youth. But, after all, these are not the surest guardians of truth.

THROUGH the life of every people winds an endless procession, which appears to totter with its feebleness, which again and again is lost out of sight among the hurrying crowd that seems to tread it under foot, and yet whose tiny hands bear safest and most pure forever the sacred treasures of all time. And if you once get a truth into the circle of that endless childhood, it makes its way to unfound hearts, and, through the crazy passions and cold bigotries of life, wins for itself an influence which men feel because they do not fear.

It was not far from the time when this Church [Trinity Church, Boston] was founded, that Bishop Butler wrote in England words which seem strange, I think, to us as we read them now. He said, "It has come to be taken for granted, by many persons, that Christianity is not so much a matter of inquiry, but that it is now at length discovered to be fictitious." And, after all that, see what life came out of what men called dead. A great many people are saying now what people used to say in Bishop Butler's day, but it is no truer now than it was then.

Life.

HERE are two souls in the world, the soul of God and the soul of man ; no other. .... The God-soul is the centre of all things. The souls of men stand around and gather all their culture and their growth from it.

No enumeration of qualities or faculties of matter accounts to us for physical vitality ; and no description of man taught and ruled and loved by God, makes clear to us that life of God imparted to man which we call holiness. Only this we are sure of, that all Spiritual Life, whether

in these its elements, or in this subtle
force which blends the elements into a
true vitality, is an inflow from the soul of
God into the soul of Man.

LIFE can only be truly communicated
by truly living methods.   Nothing else
will do.   This takes all power away from
mere machineries from the highest to the
lowest.

THAT is what we want,— strong, deep
convictions which are unshakable, and
then a glad and constant expectation of
new and richer light from God forever;
a perfect assurance of the safety of the
ship in which we sail, and then a perfect
willingness to sail into whatever new seas

God may open to us; an absolute certainty of the sufficiency of Christ, and then a passionate desire that no Christ of our own fancy may satisfy us, that He may show Himself to us more and more completely as He really is; the rock under our feet and the limitless air over our heads.

THROUGH our fathers' wisdom and devotion, we must become wiser and more devoted than they. Friends, we must rise to thoughts beyond our fathers, or we are not our fathers' worthy children. Not to do in our days just what our fathers did long ago, but to live as truly up to our light as our fathers lived up to theirs,—that is what it is to be worthy of our fathers.

THOSE be our prayers:—More strength; more light. More constancy; more progress.

THE man of the nineteenth century thinks very differently from the man of the eighteenth, but the love with which he worships God, is the same love. The Evangelical has different dogmas from the old Georgian Churchman, but they bow before the same mercy-seat, and resist the same temptations by the same grace.

A MAN is always more precious than his work.

EVERYWHERE, always, good culture

and the championship of principles belong together.

THAT men should be true to their best convictions, and to their simple duty, this is the blessing that gives all blessings with it, and is the fountain of all charity and progress.

IT is Truth that we want in every department of our life. In State and Church we need it, at home and on the street; in the smallest fashions and in the most sacred mysteries; that men should say what they think, should act out what they believe, should be themselves continually without concealment and without pretense. When we have that, then we shall have at least a solid basis of reality on which to build all future progress. It is the benefit of great and solemn crises that they give us some characters which manifest this simple Truth, that they make it to some extent the character of all the time.

ONE period collects materials, the next period builds the palace. The long, hard-working winter gathers with infinite toil the conditions of growth, stores them about the dead unanswering seed, then dies like David, and the spring-time, its successor, bright as Solomon in all his glory, comes and finds the preparation made, and, in the sunshine, builds the temple-plant.

You have seen fathers, not cultivated or educated men, who just accepted it as their task to gather the materials of a cultivated and educated life for their children. Not for them to build the gracious beauty or the massive strength of scholarly attainment; but they were content to get everything ready, and then lay the work of construction into their children's hands, in whose fulfilment of their wise ambitions they themselves should live again. And so it is in human history. Age gathers materials for age. One century with slow and painful labor beats out a few crude ideas, which lie like David's logs of wood and blocks of stone and seem merely to cumber the ground. A new century comes, and, inheriting the unfinished plan, it takes these crude ideas, and, lo, they are just what it needs. It finds

them hewn to fit each other, and out of
them it builds the compact and graceful
beauty of its institutions.

TRUTHS are the roots of duties. A
rootless duty, one that has no truth below
it out of which it grows, has no life, and
will have no growth.

MEN talk about morality as one thing,
and religion as another. Sometimes
they pit them one against the other,
as if there were some sort of natural an-
tagonism between the two. We take a
higher ground, insisting that there can
be no such thing as morality without
religion, and that morality becomes more

and more genuine just in proportion as religion becomes more and more sound and true. We do not believe in any reform which finds its whole motive within the region of human relations. We look for the permanent success of no effort, however noble its appointed aim may be, which does not draw its impulse from some association of humanity with a power and a will above its own.

WITHOUT settling detailed judgments, which it is not our place to do, we feel sure, in general, that God has bound our whole nature into such a perfect unity that no man can hold wrong opinions without incurring, just so far, danger of injury to his moral life.

ONCE accept this supreme importance of truth, and every part of our nature becomes anxious for the preservation of the testimonies of God. The great doctrines of our faith become the great pillars of our life.

ALL union between such complicated individualities as men involves surrender, the temporary stripping off of non-essentials that the essential may go on and do its work unhindered. Afterward, in the later stages of its labor, each portion of the union may resume its non-essentials, which are not therefore non-importants.

IT is the great boon of such characters as Mr. Lincoln's, that they reunite what

God has joined together and man has
put asunder.   In him was vindicated the
greatness of real goodness and the goodness of real greatness.   The twain were
one flesh.   Not one of all the multitudes
who stood and looked up to him for
direction with such a loving and implicit
trust can tell you to-day whether the wise
judgments that he gave came most from
a strong head or a sound heart.   If you
ask them they are puzzled.   There are
men as good as he, but they do bad
things.   There are men as intelligent as
he, but they do foolish things.   In him
goodness and intelligence combined and
made their best result of wisdom.

THE simple natures and forces will
always be the most pliant ones.   Water

bends and shapes itself to any new channel. Air folds and adapts itself to each
new figure. They are the simplest and
the most infinitely active things in nature.
So this nature, in very virtue of its simplicity, must be also free, always fitting
itself to each new need. It will always
start from the most fundamental and
eternal conditions, and ·work in the
straightest even although they be the
newest ways to the present prescribed
purpose. In one word it must be broad
and independent and radical.

PERFECT truth consists not merely in
the right constituents of character, but
in their right and intimate conjunction.
This union of the mental and moral into

a life of admirable simplicity is what we
most admire in children, but in them it
is unsettled and unpractical.   But when
it is preserved into a manhood, deepened
into reliability and maturity, it is that
glorified childlikeness, that high and
reverend simplicity which shames and
baffles the most accomplished astuteness,
and is chosen by God to fill his purposes
when he needs a ruler for his people of
faithful and true heart.

IT is inevitable, till man be far more
unfeeling and untrue to his convictions
than he has always been, that a great
wrong asserting itself vehemently should
arouse to no less vehement assertion the
opposing right.

WHEN shall we learn that with all true men it is not what they intend to do, but it is what the qualities of their natures bind them to do, that determines their career?

WITH a reverent and clear mind to be controlled by events, means to be controlled by God.

TRUTH and justice are in their very nature mighty and intolerant, and must fight with and conquer falsehood and sin in any region of this many-regioned universe where they may meet.

IT is not possible until the need comes, I suppose, that we should feel how legitimate and true an accompaniment of every perfect nature is Force; that is, the ability to clear its field and do its work even by the violent destruction of the hinderances that block its way.

SHALL we say that force, or compulsion, is something that is so low that it can belong to the devil only? that God can have nothing to do with it, and so that great truths and causes, high principles, which are the angels of God, his Michaels, have no right to strive; that they must not fight with their dragons? Very important it seems to me that we should understand the opposite.

THE more we see of events the less we

come to believe in any fate or destiny
except the destiny of character.

WE make too little always of the physical. . . . Who shall say that even with
David the son of Jesse, there was not a
physical as well as a spiritual culture in
the struggle with the lion and the bear
which occurred among the sheepfolds,
out of which God took him to be the
ruler of his people?

THERE is a certain wide-spread nerv-
ousness and fear of giving force any true
place in the world.   It seems a horrible
intruder, soon, we pray, to be cast out.
And yet force is as truly the companion

of reason as body is of spirit.   Righteous
force is the reaction of truth upon opposing matter.

THIS great and gracious nature tempts
me with all her alluring motherliness to
bow my will to hers and use her only in
obedience to her own laws.   But if I refuse, she flings her tempest at me, or
she sinks my ship, or scorches my un-
shielded head with her fiery suns, or
paralyzes me with disease, and compels
me back into the obedience from which
I foolishly and arrogantly tried to escape.

ANY baby may set his will against the
will of Mother Nature, and refuse to
listen to her reason ; but the most colos-

sal giant must yield his actions to her requirements and submit to her majestic force.

I CANNOT draw my picture of the perfect and perfectly effective man or state, unless I lodge the tenderest sympathy and the wisest judgment in a strong, healthy body that shall compel respect and demand obedience when the higher powers fail.

FROM his boyhood up he [Abraham Lincoln] lived in direct and vigorous contact with men and things, not as in older states and easier conditions with words and theories; and both his moral convictions and his intellectual opinions gathered from that contact a supreme degree of that character by which men knew him — that character which is the most distinctive possession of the best American nature—that almost indescribable quality which we call in general clearness or truth, and which appears in the physical structure as health, in the moral constitution as honesty, in the mental structure as sagacity, and in the region of active life as practicalness.

EVERYWHERE this earnestness of desire that truth should work, should move, should go. And what then? Why, of necessity, that if in going it should meet perhaps some obstinate resistance which will not yield, then it must break down. The brute circumstance must not tyrannize over and stop the progress of the spiritual essence.

In all the simplest characters the line between the mental and moral natures is always vague and indistinct. They run together, and in their best combinations you are unable to discriminate in the wisdom which is their result, how much is moral and how much is intellectual. You are unable to tell whether in the wise acts and words which issue from such a life there is more of the righteousness that comes of a clear conscience or of the sagacity that comes of a clear brain. In more complex characters and under more complex conditions, the moral and the mental lives come to be less healthily combined. They co-operate, they help each other less. They come even to stand over against each other as antagonists; till we have that vague but most melancholy notion which pervades the life of all elaborate civilization, that

goodness and greatness, as we call them,
are not to be looked for together, till we
expect to see and so do see a feeble and
narrow conscientiousness on the one
hand and a bad unprincipled intelligence
on the other, dividing the suffrages of
men.

Tⅲs truth comes to us more and
more the longer that we live, that on
what field or in what uniform, or with
what aims we do our duty, matters very
little, or even what our duty is, great or
small, splendid or obscure. Only to
find our duty certainly and somewhere,
somehow do it faithfully, makes us good,
strong, happy, and useful men, and
tunes our lives into some feeble echo of
the life of God.

ADDENDUM.

Chapter VIII. is taken from the columns of the *Boston Transcript;* chapter X., from those of the *Boston Herald.* The latter appeared as an editorial. The book is indebted to the *Boston Transcript* for the description of Bishop Brooks's consecration. The anecdotes and facts in the chapter entitled ''Brooksiana'' have been gathered from various sources, printed and oral.

www.ingramcontent.com/pod-product-compliance
Lightning Source LLC
Chambersburg PA
CBHW021800110726
47902CB00006B/1596